13

bluehope

bluehope

a novella | robert waldron

PARACLETE PRESS
BREWSTER, MASSACHUSETTS

Library of Congress Cataloging-in-Publication Data

Waldron, Robert G.
    Blue hope : a novella / by Robert Waldron.
        p. cm.
    ISBN 1-55725-290-4
    1. Depression, Mental—Fiction. 2. New England—Fiction.
3. Monasteries—Fiction. 4. Monks—Fiction. 5. Poets—Fiction.
I. Title.
PS3573 .A4227 B57 2002
813' .54—dc21   2001006331

10 9 8 7 6 5 4 3 2 1

Published by Paraclete Press
Brewster, Massachusetts
www.paracletepress.com
Printed in the United States of America.

In loving memory of my brother
Kevin Thomas Waldron

bluehope

Death will come like a thief in the night. That's how my depressions arrive; they descend without warning and usually in the middle of the night when I'm lying alone in bed. The first sign is rapid heartbeat, so fast I think I'm in the throes of a heart attack. Then the sweats, so profuse I must wear a towel draped around my neck. I go through several towels nightly.

Depression steals my energy, my will, and my sleep. It menacingly whispers death, but I've learned to wait it out; it eventually disappears like a mist rising from a pond. Then, I can again begin to see the contours of my life.

To find the light by which to see, I've turned to literature. Especially to poetry.

I discovered poetry in my teens. Later, it became a passion and then a way of life. Now I have a library of poets, the great and the near great. Yes, I still need the poets; they continue to illumine my life.

I opened Ethan Seegard's poetry seeking my usual sustenance, but I couldn't read. The print blurred before me, and I was too enervated to focus my eyes, attention an impossibility.

Later, I again took up Seegard and managed to read a few favorite poems, but they failed to move me. How strange and disappointing that his verse no longer inspires me. Or is it that this depression has cut too deeply for any saving word to offer its balm?

Where did I once read that depression ceases or you cease?

An evening of weeping. Deep sobs whose origin remains a mystery to me.

Today I could barely get out of bed. The third day I've not gone to work. I can't face my students' thoughtless faces and inane remarks. No doubt they're delighted I'm absent; they won't have to read poetry which, they moan, they hate. Poor fools.

My condo is quiet during the day. My neighbors all work. I hear them in the morning when they're showering and turning on the TV to listen to the morning newscast. The young woman in the condo below me drinks tea for breakfast. Every morning at seven her tea kettle whistles. I envy their normal lives.

My day is spent lying in bed, using the bathroom, and returning to bed.

Today the sun poured into my living room. I sat in an armchair and closed my eyes and felt the sun's heat. I felt better and wondered if my depression is related to light deprivation.

Wishful thinking. I've been depressed in all seasons; spring or summer light fails to disperse it. No, it's more deeply rooted than that. It's likely genetic. I once over-heard Mother whispering to Father about her great-uncle who hanged himself. She prayed I wouldn't turn out like him.

Mother referred to my depression as one of "John's moods." For hours I'd sit and stare out the window. When she'd ask me what I was doing, I'd say "Nothing." Which was the truth, for I wasn't thinking or planning or imagin-ing anything. It was like being held captive in zero, and I remembered little of what had transpired.

Occasionally Mother would become angry. With glaring eyes, she'd command, "Go out and play!" But I'd remain staring out the window, not to be disobedient but simply because I couldn't move. It was as though I were paralyzed, and only by the greatest effort of will could I gradually return to my normal routine.

This morning I washed laundry and felt soothed by folding towels, sheets, and shirts.

Tonight I cooked a meal. A simple meal but for me an accomplishment. Pasta and sauce and salad and bread. I forced myself to eat and ate most of it. The wine, however, I left untouched. Alcohol, even the mildest kind, sometimes rockets me into euphoria. It's short-lived, and I end up more depressed.

The sun rose over the Charles River. In my burgundy colored armchair, with my palms around my warm chipped coffee mug, I felt content for the first time in ages. Today I meet Paula. I know what's coming: Paula's pep talk. Although I know it by heart, I listen without protest.

Paula loves me. Unconditional love like hers isn't something I take for granted. I know how fortunate I am—such knowledge is a light that gleams, if ever so faintly, even when I'm overcome by depression.

While I walked to meet Paula, I felt my life to be so bereft of meaning that I thought of suicide. I swiftly banished the idea, but for the first time I feared I'd not live a long life.

Paula has always been there for me in my dark times. In fact, she's the only person I know who really cares about me. My parents, including my siblings, long ago stopped inviting me to holiday celebrations. I'm the weird one in the family, the mental case, the family's bad seed. My two brothers and sister are the radiant, healthy offspring who have produced three beautiful grandchildren and have made my parents so happy and so proud.

My parents had the pleasure to be proud of me when I received my doctorate in English and was quickly employed by an Ivy league college, chosen over nearly a hundred brilliant applicants. They were prouder of me when I wrote my book on the poet Ethan Seegard, nominated for the Charles Morgan Award—which I won. Yes, there were a few, brief moments when my parents were gladdened to have a son like me.

"I don't think I'll survive another depression like this one," I said. Her green eyes briefly widened. "You've said this before," she remarked, patting my hand resting on the table in Starbucks. During the academic year we'd daily meet for coffee. As usual, she urged me to return to therapy. I'd been to enough therapists to last a lifetime. I was tired, I said, of talking about being tired.

"I'm tired of hearing how tired you are. Start another project, your depression lifts when you're busy."

"I've run out of projects," I said, removing my hand from hers. Today I didn't want to be touched. "Anyway I can't seem to concentrate on anything . . . my mind wanders."

I was also in the middle of the worst semester of my professional career. My undergraduates were lazy; they sprawled before me unprepared, waiting for me to entertain them. But I refuse to be an entertainer. They got their revenge by complaints to the dean to whom they described my teaching as "boring," "out-dated," and "sleep-inducing." Dean Lavin called me in for an explanation.

Ensconced in a large black leather chair behind an immaculate mahogany desk, he said, "You must make English literature more exciting for your students." "They should already be excited if literature is their major," I said, staring at a crystal-handled letter opener.

"Things are different today, we have to motivate our students—it's our responsibility."

We argued. "If the poetry of Shelley and Keats can't excite them," I said, frustrated by the futility of our discussion, "then I certainly can't."

I looked weary, he said, and could benefit from some time off. He reminded me that I'd never taken a sabbatical and perhaps the time was ripe for one . A month of depression, I thought, had taken its toll if I look that bad.

"You'll come back rejuvenated," he said, his big, fleshy Irish face smiling. "It'll be good for you."

"How long?" I asked.

"For as long as you need."

Come back rejuvenated. What a laugh! But I agreed to a brief leave of absence and despondently returned to my apartment where I pulled down the shades, unhooked my phone, and lay in bed yearning for oblivion. Rarely would sleep, however, offer its respite of forgetfulness. At night I'd gaze into the darkness as time crawled by inch by inch. During the day I'd stare at my water-stained ceiling, remembering my father who was a roofer. He was proud of his profession. Whenever it rained, he'd go from room to room to explore our ceiling for dripping water. Finding none, he'd then proudly announce to the family, "See, no leaks." We'd all smile.

Lying in my room one day, I noticed a weakness in the ceiling. A yellow stain like a body bruise. I quickly informed Father. Peering at the ceiling, he said yes, in fact, there was a leak. Then he looked at me, and I'll never forget that look, as if somehow I were its cause.

He never repaired it. For years my bedroom companion was a large cooking pot strategically positioned on the floor to collect dripping water.

"Nothing excites you?" Paula asked, sipping her second cup of coffee. "Not even Ethan Seegard?"

"His verse no longer moves me the way it used to."

"Dear, I don't understand . . . he was your passion."

"Neither do I. Anyway he hasn't written anything in ten years. He's now living as a hermit in a Cistercian monastery somewhere in New Hampshire."

Seegard had been the most popular American poet since Frost. His books still sold but like the enigmatic J. D. Salinger, he had disappeared into New Hampshire, into solitude and seemingly into silence, for he'd published nothing after his entry into New Rievaulx Abbey.

"Wouldn't you like to meet Seegard?"

I couldn't pretend indifference to meeting the man who'd been the toast of the literary world, the poet I most admired, the poet who chucked it all for a bare, monastic cell.

"Yes, but it's impossible."

"But where there's—"

"Paula, don't say it," I pleaded, wincing from again hearing Paula's favorite cliché.

"—Where there's a will there's a way," she said, triumphantly gulping the last of her coffee while I leaked out a smile, my first in weeks. We have no doubt about our love for one another. If I asked her to marry me, I believe she'd accept me on the spot. But she wants children, and I'm not about to pass on my genes to anyone. No child of mine will suffer as I have. It would be a wanton act of cruelty.

"Love, go and meet Seegard. Perhaps that's exactly what you need."

Paula's beautiful green eyes moistened. Such a generous woman, she should've married and had a brood of happy, fun-loving kids—she'd have been a fantastic mother. Instead, she channeled her energy into her career as a professor of literature, and she was a gifted teacher. Students flocked around her, for not only was she beautiful, she was also erudite and witty. I envied her rapport with her students, one I was never able to establish with mine, frustrating because I had longed to be a great teacher like the ones who had inspired me when I was young.

"John?"

"Yes?"

"Your eyes are blue stones. I can't see you."

"The eyes are the windows of the soul?"

"Yes."

"What do you see in my eyes?"

"Can't see through stone."

"Your eyes would turn to stone too if you'd seen what I've seen."

"Describe it so I'll know." Her eyes were riveted to mine.

"I can't describe the indescribable," I said, perhaps too curtly, and averted my eyes.

"Please, tell me what it feels like."

Gazing out the window at the gray sky, I said, "It's like . . . like being swallowed by darkness."

Paula flinched and quickly lit up a cigarette; she deeply inhaled and grabbed my hand and squeezed it, "Then at least take medication."

I spared her the time I almost threw myself before a passing train. A new antidepressant opened up a fresh hell, and I thought I'd visited them all. I tossed the pills into the garbage. No pill had ever helped me and over the years I'd swallowed too many of them.

Paula stood and neatly arranged her mauve silk scarf around her neck; she kissed me and went off to teach her class on Victorian poetry. I returned home. The more I thought about Paula's suggestion about Ethan Seegard the more intrigued I became. Why had he entered a monastery? Or as I described it in my book: Why had he committed "suicide"? I had tried to communicate with him when I researched my book, but he returned my letters, saying he allowed no visitors, took no calls, and refused to entertain any questions about either his life or work. My commentary on his poetry, however, remains the standard text. What a coup, however, to write his officially sanctioned biography.

I'm convinced Seegard's poetry is the equal of the greatest moderns. But unlike them, his vision is one of bliss. He is an "ecstatic lyricist." When I first read his verse, I felt joyous and clean and saw the world as if for the first time. His poetry sustained me through my dark times, while also inspiring me to imitate his acute attention to life's beauty.

My leave of absence turned into days spent staring at the TV. With time on my hands, I realized how much I missed my students, how much I needed them. I knew they weren't lazy and useless. I likely projected my own negative feelings onto them. Intellectually I understood this, and there were times when I could muster enough objectivity to see them as they really are: young, intelligent, curious, good-hearted, and sometimes as fearful as I.

Without teaching, I was bored, and the days dragged by.

On an impulse I dialed the New Rievaulx Abbey to book a retreat. The retreat master answered the phone and brusquely said that there were no openings for six months, but he offered to put me on a waiting list; he took my phone number and address and said he'd send retreat information and hung up.

A few days later I received in the mail a brochure with a description of the abbey: "A sense of peace, palpably perceived at New Rievaulx, is its welcome to all visitors seeking union with God." It briefly described two kinds of retreats: a weekend or a seven-day retreat. I decided on the latter because I might need several days to arrange an interview with Seegard. Once inside the monastery I'd somehow meet him either by his consent or by my stealth.

Reading the brochure further, I found a poem called *The Divine Hours*. Although I couldn't say exactly what, something about the poem reminded me of Seegard. Had he reduced his verse to this ascetic line, as austere as Dickinson and as mystical as Hopkins? And if this were Seegard's poetry, then perhaps he'd been writing verse for the last ten years, adding up to several books. The hint that he'd continued to write poetry was the very fillip for my desire to journey into New Hampshire's White Mountains to meet him. So when the retreat master called the next day to inform me of a sudden cancellation, I gladly accepted the opening for a week-long retreat starting Monday, the next day.

On Monday morning I began to waver in my resolve so, before I could latch onto a reason for not going, I quickly packed essentials, put on my answering machine, and set off for the abbey.

monday

New Rievaulx is situated in a remote area of northern New Hampshire. Near the Canadian border, it is located within a valley which the French missionaries had discovered and dedicated to the Blessed Mother. The Valley of Our Lady is likely the best-kept secret in New England. With its gently sloping hills and crystalline streams, it's only a matter of time before the skiers and anglers descend upon it in droves, reducing it to another New England resort.

From Boston I traveled north four hours with one stop for coffee and the rest room. I recall little of the drive; it was as if I'd disappeared into a temporary Zen no-mind.

I came back to myself on the route to the monastery. Narrow, circuitous and seemingly interminable, it was a perilous road shrouded in fog and strewn with wet leaves.

There were no other cars. I confess the temptation. It would've been easy, so very easy to gently press the accelerator, close my eyes, and drive into the mist. A simple accident would've been the official ruling. All over in an instant. My faith would've forbidden such an exit, but I'd lost my faith in college.

I couldn't do it because I wanted to meet Ethan Seegard, to write his biography, if he agreed to it. How strange that Paula's off-the-cuff remark about Ethan Seegard had now so insistently become my raison d'être. Paula, who'd spoken the saving word, was the other reason I couldn't do it.

Somewhere along the misty, winding road I took a wrong turn, driving for an hour out of my way. Near tears—my annoyingly predictable response to life's curves—I turned into a gas station whose attendant set me on course again. The mention of New Rievaulx rendered him kind, "Ah, you're visiting the good monks . . . please say a prayer for me." I promised him one, but I hadn't prayed since college, fourteen years ago.

I drove in the direction given, the shrouded hills my only companions. I traveled a long time until I feared being lost again.

By sheer accident I noticed the small blue sign with its inscription, *The Abbey of New Rievaulx,* deliberately inconspicuous as the monks don't encourage random visitors. I left the main road for a paved lane barely wide enough for two small cars to pass. After a quarter of a mile, I shifted gears to ascend an even steeper incline and hoped my aged Toyota could make its way up without stalling.

Near the summit, I drove into a cleared space and parked near the ledge. I stared for a while into the mist, waiting for a glimpse of the valley. I hadn't realized that there were so many different hues of gray. As I was about to return to my car, shafts of sunlight pierced the pewter sky, illuminating a valley at its foliage peak: a vista of brilliant yellow, rich crimson, riotous scarlet, and bright orange. Awed by the profusion of colors, I realized why I'd always preferred autumn over spring: it tells no lies—death awaits us all.

My eyes searched for the monastery. No sign of it. I panicked. I couldn't possibly be lost. Then I saw the river, a golden ribbon meandering through the valley. My eyes followed it, hoping it would lead me to the abbey. But I saw in the distance only another wall of mist. I waited. Minutes passed before the mist arose, slowly unveiling the monastic grounds with its wide lawns, cloisters, and tower. I remembered Wordsworth's *Tintern Abbey,* a poem I loved as a teenager. Unlike the Romantic poet, I saw before me not empty monastic ruins but a living abbey.

The tower bells pealed, reverberating down through the valley. Their mellow tones were a disturbing reminder that I was still in and of this world.

I made the slow descent into the valley. As I turned a bend in the road, I glimpsed the A-framed belfry of the abbey tower, like an arrow poised toward the firmament. I parked along the circular driveway in front of the church, along with several other vehicles. The retreatants, I concluded, were a motley group: A Jaguar and a Mercedes-Benz parked alongside pick-up trucks, Chevys, and Fords.

A brick path spiraled to the retreat house with its inviting, lamp-lit mullioned windows. In the middle of the lawn stood a huge blue spruce whose branches blazed gold against the afternoon sun. I remembered a poem by Seegard about a tree transformed by the sun's radiance. I smiled, recalling Seegard's exhortation to gaze upon beauty, "Loveliness seen/Is loveliness reborn."

I rang the bell three times before a monk, in age somewhere between 30 and 50, opened the door. To guess more exactly the age of a Cistercian monk, I'd soon learn, was a futile exercise, for their way of life prolongs youthfulness. I call it the Shangri-la effect: A life of silence, solitude, good nutrition, and little stress keeps aging at bay.

Clothed in a white habit and black scapular, he eyed me through lenses as thick as a magnifying glass. I identified myself, and Father Jerome, the retreat master, shook my hand in greeting. Bearded and about five feet five, he spoke with a Brooklyn accent. His bullet gray eyes were remote and eluded my every attempt to connect, and the straight line of his pale lips didn't permit the faintest rise of a smile. I feared that perhaps he sensed my secret mission. He pointed to the room's corner to store my luggage, and I followed him through a maze of lowly lit corridors, passing through several doors and an arched sunlit cloister leading to the church. Finally at the end of the east cloister we entered the dark church through a side door. A moving shadow to my right startled me to a standstill. Jerome, on my left, touched my elbow and led me to the rear of the church and disappeared. I sat in one of the carved wooden stalls. I turned to see an illuminated crucifix hanging above the main altar, a life-sized bronze corpus nailed upon a blood-red wooden cross.

After my eyes adjusted to the dim nave, I gradually saw that I was amidst a group of retreatants seated in choir stalls that faced each other across a main aisle. How strange, I thought, that these men had found their way to this obscure monastery—to pray. I felt like a fraud. Here I was in an abbey church, pretending to be on a spiritual retreat and to believe in all this.

But the world had a right to a biography of Seegard, and I was the one to write it.

We waited for the twilight office of Vespers to begin. The silence was calming, and I breathed deeply to allow it to seep into me.

The monks began to arrive, each enfolded in a white cloud of cowl and habit. Entering the sanctuary from all directions, they seemed not to walk but to glide. Belonging to one of the oldest contemplative orders of the church, the Cistercians were founded, according to my brochure, at Citeaux, France, as a reform of Benedictine monasticism.

I looked for Ethan Seegard. When I wrote my book, I'd studied many photographs of his face in my attempt to understand the man who wrote some of this century's great verse. A tall man with angular features, he shouldn't prove to be difficult to recognize unless he'd aged terribly in the last ten years, unlikely here in a monastery.

It then occurred to me that perhaps hermits don't attend the communal liturgical hours.

Finally the abbot appeared. An elaborate gold abbatical cross hung from his neck. He had an ascetic face suffused in peace and poise. He slowly and with dignity walked to his stall where he bowed his head in prayer. When he tapped the lectern, the chanting began. I felt a rush of anxiety about telling him my real reason for coming to New Rievaulx— but what could he do, expel me?

After Vespers Father Jerome led me to my room; it was furnished with a bed, desk, lamp, bureau, and a comfortable armchair. There was also a private bathroom and a small courtyard with a view of the hills. On the wall were a crucifix and an icon of Mary and Child, and on the desk lay a schedule of the liturgical hours, a Bible, and the *Rule of St. Benedict*. Jerome wished me a peaceful retreat and departed without a smile.

I unpacked. I hung shirts and slacks in the closet and arranged socks and underwear in the bureau drawers. I placed my well-thumbed *The Collected Poetry of Ethan Seegard* atop the Bible.

All the while I was aware of the silence. Unlike the empty, sometimes frightening silence of my condo, it was a strangely peaceful silence. That there could be other kinds of silence puzzled me because silence is simply silence, which is merely a lack of sound.

I leaned out the window and inhaled the pine scented air and looked up toward the shadowy shoulder-like hills. If I could muster the energy, perhaps I'd do some hiking while I was here. The air was chilly so I closed the window and turned toward my cozy room and switched on the desk lamp with its golden light. Waiting for the dinner bell, I read the *Rule of St. Benedict*, which to my surprise I found interesting. Understanding the needs of men and the importance of work in their lives, Benedict divided a monk's day into prayer and work (*ora et labora*); they chanted the complete Psalter in about a week's time.

My life of teaching and scholarship, I decided, wasn't so very different from that of the monks. Scholarship was also accomplished in solitude and in silence. I imagined myself as a secular monk and thought how amused my colleagues would be by a such a description of our profession.

The bell clanged for dinner. I joined the retreatants in the refectory, an attractive rectangular room. Before the bay window stood a Spanish style table with intricately carved legs, displaying an autumn cornucopia of fruits and vegetables. A garland of autumn leaves encircled a large green ceramic bowl overflowing with apples. Two long tables set for sixteen people gleamed in a soft light from wall sconces. After we all assembled at our places, Father Jerome said grace and then several monks emerged from the kitchen to place our dinners before us. In silence we ate our simple meal of chicken and rice and salad while listening to a tape of Gregorian chant sung by the monks of New Rievaulx.

I poured a cup of English tea and looked around at the other retreatants and made a game of guessing their occupations. Three were obviously college students; wearing striped rugby shirts and jeans, they had unlined faces shining with youth and health. Several were well-dressed business men; others wore the harried look of blue-collar workers; one had the grease stained hands of a car mechanic. Two young, scholarly looking men sat side by side. I saw no sign of communication between them, but the darker one mysteriously knew his friend's needs, reaching out for milk or bread or butter. Then I realized that the fair one was blind.

After dessert, Jerome returned to intone a prayer of thanksgiving. He explained that it was the custom for the retreatants to clean up after meals. I washed dishes with a middle-aged man talking a blue streak. Florid and plump, Frank Higgins proudly wore the accouterments of worldly success, a diamond ring on his right hand, a rope of gold around his neck, and clothes expensive if not tasteful. Made a pile of money, he boasted, in computer software.

"It's so quiet here, isn't it?" Frank said, in a booming voice.

The men washing down tables looked up and laughed.

"Yes," I said smiling, "I assume one becomes accustomed to it."

"Have you been here before?" he asked, drying the rinsed dishes I handed him.

"My first time."

"Was New Rievaulx recommended to you?"

"Not really," I said, and decided to tell the truth and observe the reaction. "I'm here to try to meet the famous poet Ethan Seegard."

"Never heard of him," Mr. Higgins said while the others shook their heads. Except for the two young friends who became strangely still.

I returned to my room to await the bell for Compline. I sank into the armchair and wondered how I'd manage to meet the great poet. I decided to keep to my original intention and simply ask the abbot for an introduction to Seegard. With the abbot's seal of approval, surely Seegard would see me. On his part it would be an act of obedience.

He certainly couldn't find fault with me. I possessed the credentials to write his biography. Had I not written the definitive study of Seegard's verse? How could he refuse me?

Yes, tomorrow I'd spring my request on the abbot.

I took a yellow legal pad and began to write down a few questions. After making a list of ten questions, I felt satisfied. That, at least, was a beginning. But what if Seegard refused to meet me? Would he then be willing to answer my questions in writing? Surely he understands that some-one will definitely write his biography. Would he not want a person sympathetic to him and his verse, someone like me?

Imagining how he might answer my questions, I fell into a deep sleep, the best sleep I'd had in many a night and I missed Compline altogether.

tuesday

I t was the alarm clock in the adjacent room that startled me awake at 6:00 A.M. Sitting on the edge of the bed, I smiled at the absurdity of my being in a monastery, and then I slowly realized that I'd slept through the night, missing both Compline and Vigils.

I switched on the desk lamp to read the schedule of the liturgical hours:

Vigils: 3:30 A.M.

Lauds: 6:30 A.M.

Mass: 7:00 A.M.

None: 2:00 P.M.

Vespers: 5:45 P.M.

Compline: 7:30 P.M.

If I hurried I could make Lauds. I showered, shaved, brushed my teeth, threw on jeans and a sweater, and headed for the abbey. The chanting for Lauds began when I entered the church. I tiptoed down the side aisle and took the first empty choir stall I came to. All the retreatants had assembled including the blind man and his friend. When we joined the monks in singing the psalms, the blind man's voice rose above everyone's; it was a beautiful, strong tenor. A few monks darted glances toward us searching for the source of such beauty. He and his friend had become still when I mentioned Seegard's name. I thought to myself, why?

After Mass we gathered in the refectory for a buffet breakfast of eggs, bacon, home fries, juices, and cereals. I needed only coffee and to be alone. I slipped out and went into the conference room where I was taken aback by the room's rich furnishings: plush wing backs, a Persian carpet, antique tables, carved wainscoting, and a fireplace with a marble mantelpiece. Rather rich for a monastery, I thought, only later to learn that all were the contributions of a wealthy patron who believed his daughter was cured of cancer by the prayers of New Rievaulx's monks.

I sat in the corner of the room, sipping coffee and enjoying the window's view of the church near the base of a huge slope of sun-drenched fir trees. Why had Seegard, I wondered, chosen this particular monastery when he'd lived most of his life in California, whose Pacific coast had served as his muse. To a poet of his sensibility sedate New Hampshire must pale next to the grandeur of Carmel.

Soft tapping of a cane. He walked into the room and proceeded toward the couch in front of the window. He sat down and sighed. He sat ramrod straight like dancers I'd seen in restaurants near the Boston Ballet. I cleared my throat to reveal my presence.

"Sorry, am I disturbing you?" he asked, turning toward me.

"No, I'm just having my coffee. It's a beautiful room isn't it?" I said, instantly aware of the stupidity of my question.

"I like the silence of this room and it does have a beautiful feel to it," he replied, not missing a beat.

"Shall I leave?" I said, my poor attempt at a joke.

"Oh, that's not what I meant. Please don't go. In fact, I've wanted to meet you. You're here to meet the poet Ethan Seegard, aren't you?"

"Yes. You've got a good memory."

"I don't forget a voice once I hear it."

"You've read Seegard?" I asked.

He vigorously nodded his head; his profile was perfect enough to grace an ancient coin.

"Well, my brother reads him to me, and I also have his poetry in Braille and on tape."

"Your brother is the young man with you?"

"He's my twin brother."

"I'd never have guessed you were twins."

He smiled and I didn't know what else to say, although I was curious as to how he became blind. He stunned me when he said, "Degenerative eye disease. I had it but my brother was spared."

"You read minds?"

"No," he said smiling, his perfect teeth gleaming. "But people are curious and naturally wonder how I became blind."

"And your name?"

"Sorry, I'm Peter Huxley, my brother is Andrew. My mother named us after the apostles."

"I'm John Highet."

He closed his eyes as if to summon a memory.

"Are you the John Highet who wrote a book on Seegard?"

"Yes, I'm the one," I said, pleased to be recognized.

He smiled widely as if this were the most pleasant information he'd received in ages. He then complimented me on my ability to interpret Seegard.

"Your book helped me understand Seegard, but. . . . "

"But?" I said, intrigued.

"You missed the religious dimension."

"He's not viewed as a religious poet but as a neo-pagan."

"That's where your commentary fails," he said confidently. "I suggest you read Hildegarde von Bingen; she'll help you understand him."

Taken aback at being schooled by a stranger, I decided on the spot to re-read Seegard and the mystic.

"His poetry helped me to survive," he added. This was said so innocently and humbly that its melodrama was instantly deflated. "All his verse is a meditation on life's meaning."

"Are you here to meet him too?" I asked.

"Oh, I'd never violate his privacy." He stopped short. "Has he agreed to meet you?"

"He doesn't know I'm here. You obviously don't approve."

"I'm a fan of his poetry but you're a scholar. Scholars must be inquisitive . . . have I offended you?"

"No. But, be honest, you also came here in the hope of somehow meeting him, didn't you?"

He nodded and said, "Perhaps . . . but I'm really here to pray about whether or not I have a vocation . . . you're here to write Seegard's biography."

"Yes, that's my purpose. How did you know?"

"Well, it just makes sense because one hasn't been written yet."

He was thrilled by the prospect of a biography and mentioned a number of things he'd like to know about the poet, why he became a monk at the top of his list. I asked him what specifically about Seegard's poetry appealed to him. He was quiet for a long time.

"You don't have to answer," I said; "it's likely too intimate a question to ask."

He shook his head. "Not intimate, but difficult." He finally said," Seegard's verse returned to me the beauty of the world."

"I see," I said.

"That's it!" Peter said and then laughed.

"You're making fun of me," I said and laughed with him.

"No, I'd never do that," he said gently. "Seegard helped me to appreciate my senses the way he does. There are poets who help people live their lives—he's one of them."

"You and I are soul brothers," I said, agreeing totally.

"Good. I have Andrew and now I have you." He stood and extended his hand. I went to him and shook his hand. Then he took me in his arms in a friendly embrace which seemed eminently appropriate in a monastery.

"Now that we're brothers," he said, "you must tell me everything about yourself."

I told him about my life as a professor and the trials and tribulations of teaching today's students who expect to be entertained rather than taught. To my surprise I also spoke about my bouts of depression. Unburdening myself without eyes probing my face, I felt a psychological relief I'd never felt before. When I finished, he simply said, "I hope you'll be spared more suffering."

Silence.

"May I ask what first drew *you* to Seegard's verse?" Peter said.

"He's one of the happy poets, and I'm curious about the source of such happiness."

"If you could know the source, then perhaps it would be available to you?"

His remark pierced me with its accuracy.

"Yes, I believe so."

"Well, you and I aren't so different," he said, sighing. "My disability is physical and yours is psychological and poetry serves as a transfusion of strength. . . . I hope he's still writing poetry. You'll find out, won't you?"

I was about to share my theory of the authorship of *The Divine Hours* but decided not to get his hopes up.

Father Jerome appeared in the doorway to say that the abbot was ready to meet me. I excused myself and followed Jerome down the cloister. My hands trembled and my heart pounded. I nearly abandoned the whole thing, but my need to meet Seegard proved stronger than my fear.

"When he's ready to meet you," Jerome said, "Father Abbot will announce your name." He pointed to a chair outside the abbot's office, "Sit there until then." He frowned and disappeared into the abbot's office from which he emerged a minute later and without looking at me departed.

Gazing out the cloister window, I passed the time watching cloudscapes glide across the sky. Time passed and I grew annoyed at being kept waiting. I stood and knocked on the door. Nothing. I opened it and looked in to find the abbot kneeling at a prie-dieu, his head bowed in prayer. I quietly closed the door and returned to my seat.

Finally came Abbot Raine's deep voice, "Come in, John Highet."

On entering the room I met a elderly monk with watery cornflower blue eyes. "Sit down, John Highet." He indicated the chair before his desk. "Does our food agree with you?"

"Yes, Reverend Father, thank you."

"Is this your first time here at New Rievaulx?"

"Yes."

"What do you think of our home?" he asked, leaning back into his chair, his eyes probing mine. I thought of Paula and her penchant for people's eyes. The abbot's eyes, I felt, had already seen and understood too much about me.

"It's a beautiful place but I can't imagine living here."

"Then you must have a weak imagination. Here you have beauty, silence, solitude, not to mention God. What more could you ask for?"

"But I don't believe in God," I said without thinking.

He quickly leaned forward. His eyes took on a curious cast and his mouth became a thin line of annoyance. "Then why are you here if not to be in God's presence?"

I was silent, trying to decide what to say but the abbot relieved me of decision.

"It's in order to see Ethan Seegard, isn't it?" he asked, angrily.

"Yes, Reverend Father. If I requested an interview in writing or over the phone, I'd be refused. I came here under false pretenses."

My honesty seemed to mollify him; he sighed and shook his head as if he'd gone through this scene before with others.

"I'm sorry, Mr. Highet, but I must ask you to leave New Rievaulx. We are a monastery and a retreat center. Furthermore, Ethan Seegard has refused to meet visitors for ten years. He's not about to break his silence."

"You can't throw me out," I said. "I've read the *Rule of St. Benedict,* and Chapter 53 says every visitor is to be treated as if he were Christ."

The abbot laughed; he laughed so much that tears ran down his cheeks.

"You must forgive me, Mr. Highet," he said, wiping his eyes with a handkerchief, "but you are the first to have sneaked in here and thrown our rule into my face. For that I commend you."

I felt relieved. Perhaps there was a chance to meet Seegard. "You will let me stay the week?"

"Well . . . ," he hesitated, " . . . yes, how could I possibly break our own rule?"

"Will you arrange a meeting between Seegard and me?"

He abruptly stood and stepped to the window and looked out toward the hills. He was completely still, seemingly transfixed by the hills' autumnal beauty. In no small way I felt he held my future in his hands. My heart pounded so wildly I could feel its throb in my temple.

He turned to me and said, "Don't ask me why, Mr.

Highet, but I believe God, the one you don't believe in, has sent you here for a reason. I've no idea what it may be, but I shall not interfere. You are welcome here at New Rievaulx and may remain the full week. If you can somehow manage to meet Ethan Seegard, whose name is now Father Aelred, then it's fine with me; but I myself shall not arrange a meeting." He sat down and looked me in the eye, "In return I ask one thing from you . . . I want you to attend all our liturgical services."

"All?"

"Yes, including Mass. You were raised a Catholic, weren't you?"

"Yes," I said, wondering how he knew.

"You are a lapsed Catholic?"

"Yes, I guess so."

"Fine. That's all I need to know. Is it a deal?"

It was my turn to hesitate, but I swiftly calculated that there was more to be gained than lost by my staying at New Rievaulx.

"It's a deal," I said. Abbot Raines stretched out his hand and we shook. For an old man he had a firm, strong grip.

"You won't help me meet him?" I asked.

"No," he said emphatically.

"Will you tell him I'm here?"

"No, but Father Aelred's an expert in smelling out academics, as I possess a similar gift in recognizing lapsed Catholics."

I smiled and shrugged my shoulders.

"He attends Compline, doesn't he?"

Without thinking, he said, "Yes . . . oh, Mr. Highet, you *are* a clever fox. Okay, out with you and don't forget, *all* the liturgical hours. I shall be looking for you and if you're not present, I shall ask you to leave."

All the liturgical hours. So the abbot has a mission: to bring me back into the fold.

While it lightly rained outside, I sat in my room thinking about Seegard, or rather Father Aelred. A priest. What a scoop since most people believed he was one of the brothers at the abbey. How the literary world will howl with derision as they did when T. S. Eliot found faith.

Peter's remark about Seegard's spirituality intrigued me, and I decided what better place to learn about it than here in the monastery with its well-stocked scriptorium. I would speak to Jerome about using the library.

At 2:00 P.M. I attended None along with the other retreatants. When we emerged from the abbey church, we were greeted by the sun splashing through the dark sky. The valley looked like a glittering crystal bowl. The bright afternoon was an invitation to walk to the bookstore located at the monastery gate, a half a mile from the retreat house.

Along the way I noticed a leafy path meandering into the woods, and I decided to explore it. Wading through the wet, fallen leaves, I kicked aside twigs and small limbs, victims to last night's strong winds. Nature, I mused, prunes well but ruthlessly.

Across a fast-flowing stream, there was a log cabin with white smoke swirling from its chimney. A tall, thin man in jeans and a blue parka was chopping wood not far from the cabin's entrance.

"Father Aelred?" I shouted, my voice echoing through the newly rinsed air.

He instantly turned toward me. No doubt about it, it was Seegard and his face was still striking, reminding me of T. S. Eliot's sibylline good looks.

"I must speak to Ethan Seegard."

"Go away, he's dead."

"Please, it's important that I speak with you."

"Go away!" He headed toward his cabin, entered and slammed the door behind him.

Well, at least I knew where to find him, but I didn't want to press my luck by knocking on his door. Returning to my room, I sat in a state of serene satisfaction: I'd finally seen and spoken to Ethan Seegard. As far as I was concerned, I'd achieved something of rare value, and I was now more determined to interview him. Before I realized it, I articulated a prayer, "Please, let me meet him." And then I laughed: Old Abbot Raines would've been pleased.

Jerome informed me that the abbey's scriptorium was off-limits to retreatants and suggested the retreat house library. "Library" was a rather grand description for the two bookcases near the entrance. While browsing through the shelves looking for something on Hildegarde von Bingen, I heard Jerome's angry voice.

"There's a men's retreat going on and no women are allowed, so please, you must leave now."

"Listen carefully, I'm not leaving until I see John."

I entered the foyer where Father Jerome was defending the fort. "Well, here I am, Paula," I said. She wore a black wool pantsuit set off by a crimson silk scarf and looked her usual self-assured self. A few retreatants stood by enjoying the show. One of them gave me wink as if to say whoever she is she's a knockout.

"Love, I'd thought I never see you again!" she said. "And this man doesn't like women," she added, pointing her painted finger at Jerome.

"I'm enforcing our rules," said Jerome. "Our order is a cloistered one."

"Father Jerome, Miss Young and I will go into the parlor for a short visit," I said, taking Paula by the arm.

"But you must have the abbot's permission," he said.

"All right, you speak with him; in the meantime, Miss Young and I will wait in the parlor."

"Why didn't you tell me you were coming here?" she said, her voice full of accusatory concern.

"I came on an impulse. How did you find me?"

"Dear, I know you. I found out what monastery Ethan Seegard had entered and called and said your name. It was that simple."

She looked around the room and nodded appreciatively. "This is an attractive room," she said, her eyes scrutinizing the Persian rug. "Very, very nice indeed for poor monks." She sank back into a wing back and sighed. "I feel like I'm sitting in a Newport mansion. Maybe I'll stay . . . but your poor Father Jerome would have a nervous breakdown." She laughed and pointed toward the fireplace. "I hope that works, I'm chilled to the bone."

I tried unsuccessfully to ignite a blaze.

Abbot Raines appeared at the door. He was smiling.

"So you're the woman who almost gave Father Jerome a stroke!" He laughed and I was instantly relieved.

Paula stood and gave the abbot her most dazzling smile and offered him her bejeweled hand which he enfolded in his. She humbly asked permission to remain for a short visit.

"Of course you may visit," the abbot said, charmed by her graciousness. "The retreat house and the side chapels of the abbey church aren't cloistered. Father Jerome will provide coffee and a light snack for you. The only thing I ask, Miss Young, is that you not smoke." He spotted the gold cigarette case and matching lighter Paula had already removed from her purse and placed on the mahogany table.

"That will be difficult, but I promise. Thank you for your kindness," she said, glancing over at me. "John and I have a few things to straighten out."

We all smiled, but I wasn't sure why.

Jerome arrived with a tray of coffee and sandwiches. He swiftly lighted a fire, a skill, I decided, founded on years of practice. The abbot excused himself, and I heard his quiet laughter echoing down the corridor.

When Jerome left, he came close to slamming the door shut.

"He's rather grim, isn't he?"

"Yes, but only to me."

"Maybe it's not you but the human race." She smiled and embraced me and then pushed me away. "But you, taking off like that, not telling a soul—I could strangle you." She laughed and sat down to drink her black coffee.

To maintain her shapely figure, Paula ate frugally and always denied herself cream and sugar. Her reason for not giving up smoking, she'd often said, was the likelihood that she'd turn into a cow. Her husky voice was proof enough that years of smoking had taken its toll, and no amount of persuasion could convince her to have a chest x-ray. "What will be will be," she'd say, which meant end of discussion.

"Have you met Seegard?" she asked, leaning forward and precariously placing the coffee cup on the arm of the chair.

"I've seen him but I haven't met him."

"Describe him, please."

"He looks like a somebody."

"And his eyes?"

"Not close enough to tell. Disappointed?"

She smiled and reached for her cigarettes. I arched my brow.

"I know, I know . . . " and instead crossed her lovely legs and took another gulp of coffee.

We talked about Seegard and began to quote favorite lines. At one point Paula reached out to touch my hand. "I know how much it means to you to meet him. Go up to his door and knock."

"That's what I'd like to do . . . but what if he refuses to meet me?"

"Be persistent until he relents."

I laughed because that's exactly what she would do.

"That always works for you, doesn't it?"

"Not always," she said, again reaching out for her cigarettes but refraining; "It didn't work with you."

We discussed again why we couldn't marry.

Paula said, "There's no proof that your depression is genetic. Why don't you—"

"Look, we've been down this road before. Let's drop it."

"We've broken down on this road but not traversed it," she said, "but I'm here not to argue. You're all right?"

"Yes, I'm fine." I stood, "You're not driving back to Boston today, are you?"

"I thought I'd share a room here with you, if that's all right with you."

She saw my chagrin and laughed.

"We won't shock the poor, celibate monks—although I don't really think they'd be shocked. I've booked a room in town for the night," Paula said, "but before I leave, I'd like to attend Mass and one of the liturgical hours." Paula was a practicing Catholic, loved the church, and admired the Pope who, according to her, was the greatest man of the twentieth century.

We walked to the bookstore. At first, my pace was too fast. Paula was out of breath after the first incline. We slowed down and enjoyed the surrounding countryside. "This is a lovely spot," Paula said, "but the winters here must be harsh." She decided that as beautiful as New Rievaulx was, she preferred old Boston and its narrow streets.

"Why are you really here?" I asked.

"I was worried about you."

"We could've talked on the phone. No need to inconvenience yourself by driving this far north.

"I had to see you for myself. And it wasn't an inconvenience." She reached out to caress my face.

"And now that you've seen me?"

"Well, I can see you're in no danger."

"Danger?" I said, turning to her.

"You've no idea how you looked and sounded at our

last meeting. There was a desperation in your voice that I'd never heard before."

She put her arm through mine and we walked slowly, stopping often to enjoy the trees and the view of the hills. Coming toward us were Andrew and Peter. Under Paula's gaze, Andrew grew loquacious; in a short time she had his biography: He was an up-and-coming freelance artist and making a good living at it. Important exhibits in New York, Boston, and London. Mixed media: oil, water colors, and pastels. Peter remained silent but attentive. When we parted, Andrew shook Paula's hand vigorously.

"Of the two, Andrew is really the quiet one," she said.

"Well, he wasn't quiet with you. What's your magic?"

"I gave him my attention, that's all. I'll wager he didn't receive as much attention as his brother did while growing up."

"Why do you say that?"

"Are you blind?"

"No, Peter is the blind one," I said annoyed.

"Yes, and Peter is exceedingly handsome. But Andrew has a beautiful spirit."

"Peter's spirit?"

"I couldn't tell. His eyes reveal nothing. Whereas Andrew's eyes reveal everything and I saw his soul-beauty."

"You and your eyes."

"Well, dear, I do love your eyes—though sometimes they're just like Peter's— blue stones."

We were both surprised by size of the bookstore. In addition to books it also sold also jellies and jams made by the monks, and chocolates made by Carmelite nuns. Religious art was also on display. The art wasn't bad, work by the Cistercians of New Rievaulx. I found Paula standing before a portrait of Christ. It was called "The Blue Christ," a watercolor of a face floating up from blue paint. It was a miracle of execution, the result of soaking paper with water and blue paint from which emerged Christ's face. We couldn't detect any brush strokes. The brother saw us looking and said, "Brother Julian is the artist or I should say was the artist, he recently died."

"There are no brush strokes," Paula said and I confirmed.

"Yes, he moved the paint with his breath until Christ's face was fully formed. He then added a touch of crimson; he said he "kissed" it until Christ's mouth appeared. A haunting portrait, isn't it?"

We both nodded.

As we were browsing, I noticed a shelf devoted to Hildegarde von Bingen. I picked up a copy of *Scivias*. Paula looked surprised.

"Are you returning to your roots," she said, her brow arched.

"And if I am?"

"Good, it's about time."

"What does that mean?"

"It's good to know who you are."

"Thanks," I said, placing the book back on the shelf. Paula was about to say something when I raised my hand in protest. This road we had definitely traversed.

She purchased Cardinal Newman's sermons, saying his writing was the finest prose of the Victorian age. And I was not about to contradict her; here she was indeed the expert.

We walked back to her car and agreed to meet in the morning for Lauds and Mass. She was now on her way to visit an elderly aunt who lived about an hour from the monastery.

I looked forward to Compline when I'd have a closer look at Seegard. I met Peter and Andrew in the foyer; they stood next to a bookcase crowded with books on spirituality. I noticed a number of books by Henri Nouwen, Thomas Keating, Basil Pennington, and a coffee-stained copy of Kathleen Norris's *The Cloister Walk,* which made me smile for a modern woman had in fact sneaked into the cloister right under Jerome's vigilant eyes. There were a few volumes of verse but none of Seegard's.

"Peter, take my arm," I said, "and we'll go to Compline together."

"Thanks, but my brother, he—"

"Pete, I'm going ahead," Andrew said, waving us along, "you go with Mr. Highet."

Peter curved his arm into mine.

"Your friend Paula is very beautiful, isn't she?"

"Is that what your brother said?"

"Yes, and he said you were very lucky."

"Lucky?"

"To have someone like her love you."

"How does he know that?"

"Andrew's intuitive about people. He likes your friend. But—"

"But?"

"But he tends to be too susceptible," he continued, "to womanly charm and beauty."

I wondered if Paula would be flattered or annoyed by his comments.

"You're not susceptible?"

"Let me put it this way, I was too trusting when it came to women."

"Ah, I get it . . . you got hurt?"

"Enough to last a lifetime."

"You're not a misogynist, are you?"

"Of course not. My brother, however, is very naïve, and I worry about him."

"You shouldn't. He'll learn and he'll do fine."

"You're probably right. Life has a way of teaching us what we need to know."

Although I was touched by his concern for his brother, I concluded that Peter was more worldly wise than I'd previously thought.

I changed the subject by describing my brief encounter with Seegard, and even though there wasn't much to tell, Peter hung on every word.

"Please, is he as grand looking as his photos?"

"All bone and angles, very Anglo-Saxon. A sculptor would have a field day."

"His eyes?"

"You're an eye person too."

Peter kindly laughed.

"I'm sorry, I forgot," I said embarrassed. I explained to him Paula's notion about eyes being the windows of the soul.

"I sensed she was a deep person."

On entering the church, Peter took the lead as my eyes slowly accepted the low interior light. Coming to the choir stalls at the rear of the church, we separated. I went up to the first stall for a better view of the monks who sat beyond us in their own stalls. I watched the monks enter. Many of them wore their hoods up so I couldn't see their faces. In a short time ninety monks had assembled. The last to arrive was the abbot. When he tapped his stall, the chant began. As the monks sang, I noticed a late arrival who took a stall beneath a wall-sconce whose faint light was sufficient to identify him: Seegard. I had an unobstructed view of the poet all during Compline.

While the monks meditated on the psalms, I meditated on Seegard. His every movement was attentive and prede-termined even to the turning of the Psalter with his forefinger. When it was time to sit, he sat totally still and ramrod straight, the way Peter sat. He was attentive, it seemed, to everything. Even to the elderly monk next to him who kept snoozing off. Seegard would reach over at perilous leanings to lightly tap his brother's hand, and he'd snap back. I looked over at Peter and wished he could see Seegard.

At the end of Compline the monks and we retreatants formed a single line before the abbot. As we passed him, he blessed each of us with a sprinkle of holy water. I stood behind Peter and whispered, "He's here." Peter nodded.

Back at the retreat house, Peter asked for more details about Seegard, and I gladly supplied them.

"How will you meet him?" he asked.

"Tomorrow I go to his door and knock on it."

"I'd be terrified."

"What makes you think I'm not?"

"Are you?"

"Yes, but I have to do this."

"Then I'll pray for you."

I almost said don't waste your time, but his sincerity moved me and I thanked him and wished him a good night.

After last night's sound sleep, I wasn't in the least tired and spent much of the night re-reading Seegard's collected verse. It was as if I were reading him for the first time. Peter was right: Seegard's poetry was indeed a chronicle of

his search of God via beauty. I chastised myself for not seeing this. I wondered why until it occurred to me that
perhaps I was caught up in some kind of denial: I didn't see
because I refused to see. And this I would have to consider
at length.

Near midnight I fell asleep and awakened around 3:00
A.M.

I remembered my promise to the abbot and threw on a
coat and headed for Vigils. Walking across the moonlit
monastic lawns, I scanned the sky with its half-moon and
slow-moving clouds. It must be a consolation, I thought, to
believe that there was a loving God behind this indifferent
universe. And for the first time in many years I missed my
faith.

The abbey church was in complete darkness except for
the cantor's light in the middle of the oratory. A few late-
arriving monks flitted like moths toward the illumined area.
We retreatants sat together in the dark, quiet side chapel.
Peter and Andrew sat in the front pew. They sat so close
there was no space between them. Their fraternal love
touched me and I was glad that I met them. When the chant
began, I thought how bizarre it was that here were gathered
over a hundred men to sing ancient poems in a darkened
church—and at 3:30 A.M.

But what harm was there? asked an inner voice. At
least these monks lived a good, useful life grounded in
beautiful ritual and brotherly love. They were no burden to

the world because they were self-supporting. Furthermore, they offered a retreat for weary men, away from a world of getting and spending. Even I was easing into this life and already felt more relaxed. In addition to the boon of sleeping soundly for the first time in months, I felt reconnected to people.

I thought of the rest of the eastern coast. Much of New York City hadn't even gone to bed yet, the nightspots remained opened until dawn. While these men chanted to their God, others drank and danced into first light. I thought of the many other cities and their homeless, their thieves, their murderers, and their prostitutes. Under the cover of night so much of life's tragedy happens. But here in this sanctified space men devote their lives to praying for that very world.

After Vigils I returned to the retreat house craving a cup of coffee. On my way to the kitchen I passed the chapel. I peeked inside for a look and saw Andrew. I quietly withdrew when I heard my name, "Mr. Highet?"

Detecting urgency in his voice, I returned and sat down in the chair next to him. "Is there anything I can do?"

"I wish you could," he said. "But I do need someone to talk to." He relayed how faithfully he had cared for his brother for the last five years, ever since he went blind. "That's why it's so hard for me to tell him." He took a deep breath, "I'm getting married and Pete will be on his own."

"What's the problem?"

"I don't know how to tell him."

"Tell him the truth . . . he'll understand and will be happy for you."

Andrew laughed and then related the history of his brother's eye disease, the futile operations, Peter's despair, and the abrupt ending of his promising musical career as a solo pianist.

"Pete came close to giving up but—"

"You were there for him."

"Yes."

"But he's over that now and seems well-adjusted."

Andrew gave me a look that said you don't know the whole story. But I already knew more than I wanted to know. I wasn't good at carrying other people's woe; it tapped into my limited amount of psychic energy which at an early age I had learned to husband.

"Tell him. There's no way to evade it."

"I'm afraid you're right, but—"

"Yes?"

"He'll be sad."

His guileless remark almost made me smile.

"Why?"

"He'll be alone."

"We're all alone, Andrew," I said, thinking of my siblings with whom I hadn't spoken in two years. "No one escapes that."

He looked at me in disbelief and then shook his head. I felt certain that he felt quite as sorry for me as I for him.

"On the other hand, if it turns out Peter has a vocation, then your problem is solved. He won't be alone but a member of a community."

Andrew looked relieved and smiled. As I walked away, I felt his eyes following me. I left him, envious of the closeness he shared with his brother. My brothers and sister and I were never close. They were afraid of my bouts of depression, and thus kept their distance. But even if they had reached out to me, I wonder if I would've accepted their concern.

wednesday

I met Paula as she was getting out of her car. She gazed up at the hills and the morning sky streaked in mauve, orange, and gold.

"It's beautiful here. The air is delicious." She looked up at the abbey tower. "A beautiful place, isn't it?" I found myself nodding.

We attended Lauds seated in the guests' chapel, which we had to ourselves. The retreatants had assembled at the rear of the nave which was cloistered. The candlelight, the clouds of incense, the moving white shapes of cowled monks, the singing, all of it enchanted Paula. "It's like being in another world," she whispered, smiling. When she went to the altar to receive Communion, I felt like an uninvited stranger at a family gathering. For the first time in years I felt I'd perhaps rejected something good and worthy.

On our way back to her car, Paula was nostalgic, "As a girl I loved going to church. Every Sunday our family attended the ten o'clock High Mass. Father, Mother, my three sisters, and me. After Communion I'd feel so pure and serene, and if on the way home I died, I'd go straight to heaven. I even entertained the idea of becoming a nun . . . but what Catholic girl didn't in those days?"

"You a nun!" I exclaimed, chuckling.

"I know, it sounds ridiculous," she said, "in light of what I've become."

"What you've become! Paula, you've *become* a warm, loving, caring woman who drove hours into the boondocks to see me. I love you for it." I hugged and kissed her.

"Thank you for saying that. But it's so strange," she said, lost in a distant memory.

"What's strange, Paula?" I prodded.

"That my first love affair was with God." Morning sunlight glimmered in her tears. I hugged her again, thankful for her presence in my life.

She urged me to return to teaching. As to what was down the road, she was realistic, "Dear, please don't hesitate to call me—for anything. I'm always here for you."

"I'll never understand why you bother with me, why you care."

"Because I *choose* to care . . . and it's my decision."

"I've no say in this?"

"No," she said with a finality in her voice that meant end of discussion.

We kissed, and she drove off and I watched her car until it disappeared around the bend.

At breakfast I sat with Peter and Andrew. I enjoyed talking with them. They were unmasked, totally themselves. They were the opposite of so many of my students who'd adopted poses but never seemed able to drop them.

Andrew's attention darted back and forth between Peter and me, while every once and a while brushing off toast crumbs from Peter's shirt. When he left to clean up the kitchen, I expressed to Peter my misgivings about my book on Seegard.

"You're being too hard on yourself. Your commentary is perfect as an introduction to Seegard."

"But I missed so much of the religious dimension. As a scholar I should've seen."

"May I ask a personal question?"

"Certainly."

"Do you believe in God?"

"I used to."

Peter slightly nodded as if my answer confirmed his already formed opinion.

"Maybe you can't see what you no longer believe in."

"That's no excuse. The clues were there . . . you did."

He sighed and said, "But I believe." His remark wasn't accusatory, but I had the distinct impression that he felt sorry for me, and I wanted no one's pity.

"Belief or no belief, I should've seen that he is essentially a mystical poet."

"Maybe it's time for you to rewrite your commentary; other critics have done the same."

"That's a big piece of humble pie."

"Food for the soul."

"But I don't believe—"

"In the soul?"

We both laughed.

"What *do* you believe in, John?" Peter asked suddenly.

"I don't know. Maybe that's why I'm here . . . to find out."

I was surprised by my remark because I'd convinced myself I was here simply as a scholar who wanted to meet Seegard. To be driven also by a hidden agenda hadn't occurred to me—until now.

It was a perfect fall day. Sunlight stippled the surface of the stream, and a breeze swayed the trees' branches. I sat myself on a large rock and spied on Seegard's hermitage, trying to muster the courage to knock on his door. Near noon he emerged and headed toward a mound of logs to embrace an armful and disappeared inside. Smoke soon curled its way from the chimney.

After a while I felt a bit foolish sitting on a stone like Buddha under the Bo tree with Seegard's *Collected Poetry* by my side. Americans had become infamous for their voyeurism, and now I had joined the ever-growing pack. But I was a scholar, I consoled myself, with the right to study Seegard's life. As for Seegard's privacy: When he accepted the Pulitzer and Lamont Prizes, fame became a fact of life, and he'd have to live with the consequences.

I opened his poetry and read, "Lift your eyes from the gilded missal/And behold the earth's munificence." As a poet he seemingly disparages his art. You won't find what you seek, he implies, in a book no matter how profound its beauty. Yet had I not found courage and beauty in his verse? Hadn't his poetry inspired me to see the world's loveliness? Hadn't his joy in beauty become my own?

I closed the book, determined it was now or never. I jumped the stepping-stones across the stream, from one slippery rock to another, inadvertently dipping my shoe into the water. With my foot soaked to the skin, I stood safely on the other side before his cabin. My heart pounded. "This is crazy," I thought, but I summoned the last of my nerve and walked up to his door and knocked.

"Go away!" he bellowed from inside.

I knocked again.

"Go away!"

I felt like a fool. I was about to knock for the last time when the door opened. Tall and imposing, he glared at me with eyes nestled in a squint of fine wrinkles.

"Are you deaf?"

"I need to speak with you."

"I need silence. Whose need is greater, yours or mind?"

"You're a priest, where is your charity?"

He slammed the door. From inside, "Go away now!"

I returned to the retreat house, cursing at every turn all priests and monks. I found Peter in the conference room. Wearing earphones, he was lost in a world of music. I shook his shoulder. "Yes?" he said, quickly removing his phones.

"Your icon slammed the door in my face!"

"Oh, so now he's my icon and not yours?" he said, quietly laughing.

"It's not funny. He was downright rude."

"More rude than your uninvited self?"

I sat down in my usual chair and breathed deeply to calm myself. After a few minutes I said, "Well, I've wasted a lot of time coming here, so I'd best start packing and return home."

"You're giving up rather easily, aren't you?" Peter said.

I wanted him to think well of me. "I did the very thing I was terrified to do."

Peter gently asked, "What terrifies you now?"

"More humiliation. I couldn't knock on that door again if my life depended on it."

Silence

"Give him one more chance," Peter said with feeling.

"I threw his priesthood in his face and he didn't flinch."

"Why not tell him who you are?"

"I didn't have a chance!"

Peter was quiet. I couldn't tell if he were annoyed with me or simply disappointed.

"Peter, say something."

"Okay. Try one more time."

"Why should I?"

"Seegard's important to the both of us and who knows how many others." He paused. "And you need him."

"I don't need him or anybody for that matter."

Silence.

"I don't believe you," Peter said, turning toward me. His blind eyes stared at me, and I had an eerie feeling he could see me.

"We all need each other," he said quietly, "have the humility to accept it. If my blindness has taught me any-thing, it's that."

He was right. I needed to speak with Seegard.

"And have the courage to face your despair." He rose and left the room before I could respond.

Despair? Was I in despair? Surely he's not confusing my depression with despair. I knew enough about the inner life to know that for many people the antidote to despair is faith. Or so said Father Flynn, my high school English teacher. He explained that T. S. Eliot was a man in despair when he wrote *The Hollow Men*, but by the time he composed the *Four Quartets*, he was a man of faith and hope.

By my junior year of college, I'd lost my faith. It all comes back clearly. I was enrolled in Professor Jeremy James's modern poetry class when he lectured on Eliot's *The Waste Land*. Responding to one of his questions, I alluded to my Catholicism. James arched his-brow and said, "A Catholic, how very quaint." Other students laughed. I blushed.

James was a gentleman: silver hair, tailored suits, clipped diction. A close reader of the text, he dazzled us with his interpretations of Eliot, peppering his lecture with witty asides about the modern literary scene. He was quite popular with students who surrounded him and believed his every pronouncement. And he pronounced on everything. I know because I was one of his devotees.

Had I tossed away my faith to win his high favor?

Surely my lack of faith has no link with my depression. Perhaps that's what Peter thought he'd detected. Although depression and despair may superficially look similar, they're quite different. The former is debilitating, the latter is often fatal. The former you can live with, the latter murders.

Am I in despair? No, I'm simply a man without faith. An often depressed man, yes, but I've lived with it and will continue to do so.

But why do I find myself—go ahead, say it—why do I find myself wanting to believe in God again?

A knock on my door. I opened it to find Seegard's blue eyes burrowing into mine. Astonishment fails to describe my reaction. Lank and spare, he was the portrait of an El Greco-like ascetic. He gave the impression of a man supercilious to all that's extraneous.

"May I come in?" he asked in a deep, finely modulated voice.

I nodded and stepped aside to allow him to pass. I tried to appear poised when I actually felt faint.

"May I sit?"

He took the desk chair. His presence filled the room. I remained standing, not knowing what to say or do or where to look, for I couldn't hold his gaze very long.

"Sit down, please," he said, more like a command than a request. "I've spoken to the abbot about you. Concerning you he says I may do whatever I please, but he also reminded me that we should treat all visitors as Christ and today I failed at that. Please accept my apology."

"Apology accepted," I said, perhaps a bit smugly because I detected the slightest double take in his eyes now searching my room and briefly lingering on my volume of his verse.

He looked at me, "What can I do for you?"

"I'm John Highet," I said as if that explained it.

"The Highet who wrote *The New Poet of Carmel*."

"Yes."

He smiled. I took it as a positive sign. His rough hands smoothed out the wrinkles of his white habit. He took a deep breath and said. "What is it you want?"

"A long interview with you and your blessing to write your biography," I quickly said before I lost the courage.

His bellow of laughter surely echoed throughout the retreat house.

"You're a cheeky fellow! By the way I don't like your description of my vocation. If I remember correctly you said it was suicidal. Becoming a monk, Mr. Highet, is the bravest thing I've ever done."

"How?"

His eyes squinted. "His Reverence said you're a clever fox. No questions now, but I'll grant you one interview. As to a biography, after all these years is there really enough interest to warrant one?"

"Ten years of absence has made you the Garbo of poets."

He roared again.

"So people are still reading me?"

"Yes, and there's a young man here who's blind . . . he says your verse saved his life."

He frowned and shook his head as if this disturbed him so I refrained from telling him about my own similar feelings. Anyway, scholarly objectivity would more likely win him over than gushing adulation.

He stood and said, "I'll give you time. Jerome will tell you when to come."

"Where?"

"My cabin."

I stood to offer him my hand, but he'd already turned and opened the door and disappeared down the hallway. Just as well, my hand was a wet rag.

After lunch I found Peter in the conference room.

"I'm meeting the abbot today to discuss my postulancy," he said, his face flushed with excitement.

I found myself smiling; Andrew's dilemma might now be solved. I hoped Peter was entering the monastery for the right reasons and not to find a safe haven from a too frightening world.

"Does one choose to be a contemplative?" I asked.

He was silent for a long time, and I feared I may have sounded flippant.

"I'm not sure," he said at last. "Maybe one's born a contemplative. Or maybe one is called to be one . . . I'm not sure."

His struggle to answer my question, perhaps an unfair one, was endearing, and I liked Peter the more for it.

"Tell me how it all began?" I said, my attempt at rescue.

"After a grueling piano competition, I needed poetry, you know, food for the soul, so I decided to re-read Shelley, my favorite poet. At the library, I was reaching for Shelley when another volume among the "S's" fell into my hands, Ethan Seegard's *Radiance* . Right there in the aisle his verse possessed me."

I laughed at the amusing image.

"You know what I mean," he said smiling. "The surprising thing about Seegard's verse is that he believes that we all have the potential to be contemplatives, that one needn't be a saint."

"Your interest in contemplation occurred before your blindness?"

"Yes. But when I got caught up in my music career, I put my spiritual life on the back burner."

"Faith is no problem for you," I said. "You whole-heartedly believe in God?"

"Yes, of course I believe in God, but faith is always a problem," he replied, taken aback by my question.

"How?" I asked, now considering people of faith to be exotic creatures. Except for Paula, all my colleagues were either atheists or agnostics.

"Because belief doesn't completely satisfy the intellect . . . one never knows God, one believes in him." He took a deep breath and smiled, pleased that he'd articulated an idea he'd seemingly never expressed before.

"You believe you can experience God?" I asked.

He shifted his position in his chair, placing his right foot beneath his left ankle. My question disturbed him; he finally said, "Yes, or rather I hope to experience God. If I never experience God directly, like the mystics, I still believe in him."

"Why did you choose to come here?"

"I made a retreat here and felt it was a holy place."

"Felt?"

"I know it sounds like something from a romantic novel, but I felt what I can only call holiness the first moment I arrived here. And I knew I'd found what I'd been searching for."

"And Seegard's presence here?"

"A nice coincidence."

We both fell silent. He was comfortable with silence, and I felt no compulsion to speak. As if silence were a social gaffe, I'm often the first to insert pregnant pauses with non sequiturs.

"I've something to tell you too," I said but then fell silent, waiting for him to take the bait.

"Oh, come on, spill it." he said, amused by my little game.

"Only if you're interested in Ethan Seegard."

He smiled, and I described Seegard's brief visitation three times before he was satisfied.

"This is a dream come true, isn't it?" Peter said.

"Yes. I never thought I'd meet him face-to-face and shortly I will interview him."

"You must find out if he's still writing and—," he paused.

"And?"

"Please ask him about his vocation . . . how he knew for sure he had one."

"Already having doubts?"

"I want to be certain I'm not doing this to unburden my brother."

"Do you think you're a burden?"

He was silent, his eyes glimmering with tears.

"Peter?" I asked gently, afraid I'd gone too far.

He turned toward me as if he'd forgotten me; his face

turned crimson. "Sometimes I feel I'm keeping Andrew back. He has a right to his own life. Anyway, please ask Seegard how he knew he had a monastic vocation—it could be helpful to me."

I promised.

On my desk I found a note from Jerome indicating that I was to meet Seegard at 10:00 A.M. in Seegard's cabin. He underlined "Be prompt!"

thursday

arrived at his hermitage at exactly 10 A.M.. As he prepared tea, I looked around. Although small, it had a
living room, kitchen, bedroom, and bathroom. The kitchen
had a table, two cane chairs; the bedroom a single bed,
desk, and one bureau. No TV, radio, or telephone; and it
was spotlessly clean, with the fragrant smell of cedar wood
permeating the air.

Against the living room wall was an altar for Mass,
above the altar on the wall a copy of Rouault's *Man of
Sorrows*. A crimson and white rug with an American native
design along its edges lay on the floor before the altar. A
small wooden box on the wall to the left of the altar served
as a tabernacle.

As he poured tea, I began to talk uncontrollably, pouring forth everything about my lifelong battle with fear and
depression. One swift unburdening of the heart. When I
finished, I was soaked in sweat. And utterly mortified. I
immediately apologized. "This abbey has had a strange
effect on me," I said, as an offer of some explanation.

"Yes, it can do that," he said, staring at his hands. After

a long silence, he said, "My wife suffered from depression . . . but you must fight it, never give up. Find that which gives hope. My wife—"

He shook his head, clearly dismissing from his mind a pained memory. I wanted to hear about his wife. He spoke instead about how long it took him to persuade the abbot to build the hermitage. He'd deliberately chosen a safe subject. "There are now two hermitages within the monastic enclosure," he said proudly, "and the abbot has often availed himself of the other." He talked about the advantages of the eremitical life.

I was determined, however, to discuss his poetry. I said, "Your verse is imbued with joy. What's the source of such joy?"

He raised his eyebrows as if amused by my sudden boldness.

"When I was joyful, I wrote about it—quite simple."

"But the source?"

"Look, there is no reason for joy, if that's what you mean. It arrives. And I try to capture the lingering memory of it to share with others . . . and to remind myself. See, in the beginning it's beyond thought and demand . . . it's like grace."

"I don't understand."

"You've read my poetry?"

"Yes, but I never plumbed the mystery of—"

"Of my being? Is that what you're here for, to plumb the mystery of my being? You poor fool!"

He laughed and I was hot with shame.

He went to the two-burner hot plate to boil water for a second cup of tea; pouring two mugs, he again sat across from me.

"Why not try to understand the source of your depression."

"I'm sorry I mentioned it," I said, afraid of alienating him, "I've never spilled my guts like that to anyone."

"Confession is good for the soul."

"I'm not confessing anything," I said, annoyed that he might think I sought spiritual advice.

"Aren't you?"

"No. I'm sharing with you the fact that out of nowhere this inexplicable sadness overcomes me."

He shrugged his shoulders and said, "Then you must find its cause. Self-knowledge is a journey we all must embark upon."

He'd turned the tables on me. Here to discuss him, we were talking about me.

"That's not to say, Mr. Highet, that there won't be people along the way to help you," he said. "I was fortunate to meet—to meet one or two who pointed me in the right direction when I was lost." He was again deliberately vague. Referring to his wife, perhaps? He'd married a woman half his age who died of leukemia not long after their marriage. Had he himself become a monk for the wrong reason, to escape an agonizing grief?

"Your verse went everywhere with me," I said, steering him toward his poetry.

He smiled and shook his head in disbelief. "That's kind of you to say."

"It's got nothing to do with kindness," I said angrily. "Your poetry was a lifeline."

He sipped his tea and again shook his head incredulously.

"Your becoming a monk wasn't fair to your readers," I said. "It was like cutting off a faithful and true friend."

His lips disappeared into a thin line and his right hand closed into a fist. I hit a nerve and I was glad.

He said, "See . . . I'm not by nature a gentle man."

"You could've fooled me," I said. He frowned, his hand relaxed, and then he slowly smiled. I felt I'd finally broken the ice.

"When I realized my lack of gentleness, well, it was a shock—as self-knowledge often is." His voice was quiet and filled with pain. "I hurt a young man. I crushed him until the pith burst the rind and I shall never forgive myself." He paused. "He wanted to be a poet."

"Poets are sensitive," I said, commiserating, "and should develop a tough skin."

"This was different. See, the man whose verse I mauled committed suicide soon after our meeting. To me that's the most tragic act—to take one's life. My insensitivity about his verse pushed him to the edge."

He remained quiet as if reliving the experience. His silence wasn't comfortable like that which I felt with Peter. Then to my utter shock, I felt him grab my hands, "Promise me you'll never take your life."

Terrified that he'd seen into my deepest self, I felt sweat beading on my brow.

"You've no right to ask me that," I said, pulling my hands away from him. "My life's my business and no one else's."

He stood and triumphantly looked down at me. "I fully agree with you, Mr. Highet, and my life is *my* business and no one else's."

"But it's different, you're a public man."

"I'm no longer a public man."

"You can't escape your fame."

"Fame?"

"You've no idea of your fame?"

"Explain, please."

"Salinger is now more famous because he too is holed up somewhere in this state. Same with you, and you've got to accept it."

He sat down. A look of defeat spread across his pale face. As he gazed at his folded hands, I felt pity for him.

"I came here to disappear into God," he said, lifting his eyes to mine. "I don't want fame or anything the world offers."

"You hate the world?"

"Let's say I distrust it."

"Then your being a monk is a failure."

"Why?" he said, startled.

"Isn't religious life founded on love of God and neighbor?"

He stood.

"I'm tired," he said, "and ending this now."

"You promised me an interview."

"And I'm a man of my word . . . return tomorrow, same time," he said, moving toward the hearth. "I'm fresher in the morning; it's when I do my best writing."

"You do write."

Angry with himself for this slip of tongue, he too vigorously threw a log onto the fire, spitting sparks everywhere.

"You may go, Mr. Highet."

I detected a tinge of friendliness in his voice.

As I passed through the door, I heard, "Don't be late."

Excited and needing to talk to someone, I was on my way back to the retreat house when I was stopped by a van of tourists, two elderly men up front and two women in back.

"What is this place?" the driver asked. I detected a Canadian accent.

"A monastery."

"What's that?"

Was he pulling my leg? His face was as deadpan as Buster Keaton's.

"A place where monks live."

"What do they do?"

"Nothing."

"Nothing?"

"They pray."

He nodded as if he fully understood.

"Are you a monk?"

"No."

"Then why are you here?"

I wanted to escape from my inquisitor so I coldly said, "I'm here to enjoy the silence."

"A lot to be said for silence."

Was this guy for real? Was there the slightest of smiles? He revved up the van and advised me to "eat up that silence," and off he went with his hand out the window waving good-bye. I found myself feeling quite happy about this bizarre exchange and blithely went in search of Peter and Andrew.

Father Jerome informed me that the retreat group was watching a video on the Cistercian way of life. He invited me to attend, but I decided to visit the abbey church whose quiet I'd found peaceful; it was also a good place to think. As I entered the cool darkness, I was instantly enveloped by silence. After my eyes agreed to the dimness, I looked around to find the church empty. I sat in one of the monks' choir stalls. The wood was cool to my hand.

The stained-glass windows' blue-gray light illuminated the side aisles only to fade into the shadow of the middle aisle. The flickering red vigil lamp on the altar whispered the presence of Christ in the tabernacle. If truly present, I thought, Jesus would be aware of me, looking directly at me. What would he say to me sitting here alone in a choir stall? What would I say? Perhaps there'd be nothing to say. Perhaps silence would be enough.

And Seegard? With him silence wouldn't do. There were too many questions I needed to ask. Questions to be carefully framed and artfully articulated. His remark about gentleness, surely this is pivotal and must be explored. Who was the young man who took his life?

He still wrote poetry. Ten years would add up to quite a book or books. He'd obviously exhausted the muse of Carmel. But how had the tame hills of New Hampshire spoken to him? Maybe his verse would surprise everyone, the way Wallace Stevens's late poetry stunned the literary world.

The silence was suddenly ended by organ music, rising and falling like the surge of the sea. Glorious music. Listening, I felt as if I were privy to someone's inner life. The music soared to the heights of joy, and without warning it plummeted to the depths of sorrow, of despair. Thereafter arrived a slow crescendo, a ponderous, painful climb from the slough of despair toward acceptance, toward serenity, followed by a stately movement into further crescendo . . .

and then sudden, swift flight into joy and beyond that into ecstasy.

I'd forgotten where I was when the music abruptly ceased, startling me.

"Who's there?"

I recognized the voice. "Is that you, Peter?" I said into the darkness.

A circle of yellow light blazed when Peter switched on the organ reading lamp. He sat erect on the bench with his face toward me. As I went toward him, I said, "Were you playing Bach?"

"No, it's my own transcription of a Beethoven sonata . . . Father Jerome said I could try the organ. If I am accepted into the order, I'll likely be one of the organists." As I praised his talent, Peter warmed to it and began to reminisce about his life, about how his talent had been spotted when he was quite young and how his parents sacrificed so much to employ the best teachers both in America and abroad. He won several international competitions and was considered a rising star in the music world.

He was on his first concert tour when his eyes began to trouble him. At first, it was a brief blurring of vision caused, he surmised, from reading too many musical scores. An eye examination detected nothing serious, and glasses were prescribed. His vision, however, continued to deteriorate. Then there were periodic blackouts when he couldn't see anything.

"Something was terribly wrong, and I finally went to a specialist who said I'd lose my sight within a year. My music career was over."

"Why over?"

"Do you know any blind concert pianists?"

"No. But you could be the first."

"The competition is too fierce, and I didn't have the will to abide in that world. I had to battle my own fears. That's when Seegard's poetry came to my rescue. He opened my eyes for the first time, and I voraciously drank in the world before my sight faded away forever." He paused and said, "But that's all in the past. Now I'm more concerned about my future."

He didn't say anymore, but he reached out and took my arm. I was touched by his trust in me. As we made our way back to the retreat house, I described my meeting with Seegard and my hunger to know more about his life.

"Please, John, I must meet him. Will you ask him?"

"Of course."

He squeezed my arm in thanks.

At Compline I watched the cowled monks as they entered into the nave of the church. Their white movement floating through the darkness reminded me of an abstract painting I'd admired in the New York Metropolitan, simply titled *White Against Black*.

The monks began to chant Psalm 4.

O Lᴏʀᴅ, let the light of your countenance shine
> upon us!
You put gladness into my heart,
> more than when grain and wine abound.
As soon as I lie down, I fall peacefully asleep,
> for you alone, O Lᴏʀᴅ,
> bring security to my dwelling.

> (Psalm 4:6–8 ɴᴀʙ)

These monks must be consoled, I thought, to know that for over nine hundred years somewhere on this earth their order ended its day praising and thanking God. Intercessory prayers followed for the elderly, the sick, the imprisoned, the suicidal, the tortured, and to my surprise, for those suffering from depression. Synchronicity or had Seegard spoken to someone?

A young monk slowly ascended the marble steps of the main altar to light two candles on each side of the tabernacle. The stained glass window of Mary and Child high above the tabernacle wavered in candlelight until a switched-on light from outside flooded the jewel-like colors of the glass icon. Like moths attracted to flame, every monk's attention was riveted to this portrayal of Mary. They slowly sang the *Salve Regina*, slowing down even more to intone the last verse, "*O clemens, O pia, O dulcis virgo Maria.*"

At the end of the service, we all approached the abbot in single file for his blessing with holy water from a aspergillum. When my turn came, the abbot put his hand on my bowed head, whispered a prayer, and with three strong flicks of his wrist he soaked me with water. I immediately thought he'd accomplished some benign revenge for my coming here under false pretensions. Or knowing the state of my unbelieving soul, he perhaps thought I needed to be rebaptized a Christian. I looked at him for a telltale sign, but his face was inscrutable.

On my way back to the retreat house, I paused to gaze at the vastness of the night sky and its wafer moon. I wondered about the countless people who had gazed upon this celestial infinity. Some saw gods, others mystery. I saw my own insignificance. Shaped like shrugged shoulders, the dark hills served as the monastery's last barrier to the outside world, and I wondered how long the monks could maintain their solitude.

I turned toward the woods where in a shaft of moonlight I saw a hooded figure walking down a path. Seegard returning to his hermitage. I shuddered. Perhaps I was expecting too much of him. Over the years, I had built him up in my mind, leaving no room for frailty. And now what if I find out my icon has feet of clay?

friday

When I arrived at his hermitage, Seegard had completed Mass and was helping himself to a cup of coffee. I sat down at the kitchen table, accepting his offer of toast and coffee. He talked more about the history of the hermitage. The first hermitage had been an abandoned shed once used to store plows and other farming tools.

"At first the novices would sneak out there to meditate and then I started to use it. It had a stove and a bed. The abbot let me stay overnight. I kept badgering him for more solitude until he caved in and built this."

He took me out back and pointed to a small hut.

"That used to be the outhouse. There was a snake nesting in there, and it used to scare the hell out of me. One day I threw a rock at it, and I felt quite bad about it afterwards—such a paltry act—and it slithered away into the underbrush. Now we're quite modern with indoor plumbing . . . but there are times when I miss the good old days, like when I washed everything in rain water."

We sat in front of the hearth with its small blaze.

"As a young poet, did you have a mentor?"

"In the plural—poets of the nineteenth century, and modern poets like Jeffers and Rilke."

"No mentors that you knew personally?"

"In the singular, my wife; she was the best teacher I ever had . . . I loved her very much.

"How often she and I were simultaneously captured by the same beauty, a swaying tree, an unusual cloudscape, or a flower of rare coloration. Then the subtle, silent assent, 'You too?' Such moments gently descended upon us. Or they arrived suddenly, jerking us out of ourselves into an acute attention upon a slant of light or bird flight or leaf patterns reflected on the grass. Or over a cup of coffee at four in the morning when we'd both listen to the night's silence, aware of a pulsating presence on the brink, we felt, of bursting into a Big Bang of revelation, transforming our lives forever. Exquisite moments.

"What we had was miraculous. We never spoke about our moments of communion. Somehow we both suspected the spoken word might mar or debase them. Strange, isn't it, that being poets we feared language, but we believed in the ineffable and our every verse was a new attempt to capture its mystery."

After he and Anne had married, they continued to live in Boston where they taught at different colleges. He described academia as cutthroat and heartless. He longed to live simply and peacefully in the country. His wife had been raised not far from New Rievaulx and had never taken to Boston and its snobbery toward outsiders. When a farm near New Rievalux came up for sale, Seegard quickly purchased it.

"My wife had known the monks since she was a girl, and she introduced me to them. Of course, she was twenty years younger than I so I don't think they at first approved of me. But I didn't care because I saw how much they loved her."

"Was she religious?"

"She loved her church but she loved—"

He paused, and I sensed his weighing whether or not he should tell me such intimate details about his life. I held my breath, afraid to destroy the moment with an inane comment or one that would annoy him.

"She loved Christ . . . my only rival. That sounds almost absurd, doesn't it?"

"It is if you didn't believe in Christ," I said.

He quickly looked at me.

"You are clever, Mr. Highet. You're right, I didn't believe in Christ . . . well, let me qualify that. I didn't believe in God."

"An atheist!"

"An agnostic," he replied, his gnarled hands enfolding his coffee mug.

"Do you believe in God now?"

He was silent too long, and I feared I'd perhaps gone too far. But then he continued.

"Here God was present to me."

"So, you believe in God?" I persisted, surprising myself.

"We're not talking about my belief, are we?"

I shifted my gaze from his face to my hands.

"Your silence is eloquent," he said, shaking his head in pity, annoying me to no end.

He went into his bedroom and came back with a sheet of paper.

"Something special?" I asked, sensing he wanted me to ask.

"Anne composed this a week before she died. Her birthday gift to me; she was so pleased, so happy. She was a far better poet than I, but it's a man's world. Her brief life and my long one—it's all such a mystery."

He was 63.

I read the poem, a touching one about her and her mother praying the rosary after dinner while washing the dishes, how they were never closer than when reciting the Hail Mary.

"Beautiful. You miss her. Don't you?" I said, handing back the poem.

"Of course."

He stood up. "Come, it's too beautiful a day to be cooped up in here."

He led me on a tour of the monastic enclosure. Like any man proud of his home, Seegard pointed out the renovations to the abbey's bell tower, the vast extent of New Rievaulx's holdings, including ponds, streams, and farmland; we passed the new jelly factory, a small, square red-brick building.

Ethan Seegard's attentiveness was infectious, and he commented on everything: the cloudless sky, the autumn sunlight, the curlicue of tree shadows on the grass, the chipmunk totally still as we passed it—all possessed a particularity of beauty he joyfully savored and shared.

We arrived at a wooden bench, both of us glad to sit.

"When I was a novice I built this bench for old Father Dominic, who loved to sit here in the warm weather and meditate." Seegard gazed at the panorama of hills, in the finale of their autumn beauty.

"Mother Nature exits not with a whimper but a bang," he said pointing toward the hills. "Amazing how some leaves cling to the branches. Another storm will lay the last to rest."

"Do you often come here?" I asked.

"I used to. Over the years I've had beautiful moments here . . . yes, my eyes were opened here."

"To anything in particular?"

"My need for silence and solitude. I wasted too much of my life in the pursuit of—well, to be truthful, fame."

"But most writers hope to be famous."

"Yes, perhaps. But that's not the purpose of art."

"What is its purpose?"

He looked at me and smiled.

"Did I say something amusing?"

"No. I'm smiling because you're asking the kinds of questions that used to send me into a fury. See, I've always had a temper; it's one of my crosses."

"So what is the purpose of art?" I persisted.

"Mr. Highet, I've just told you."

"Temper, temper," I said, without thinking.

"Thank you for the reminder," he said. After a long pause, "Art helps us to search."

"To search?"

"Yes . . . or rather it's the beauty of art that helps us in our searching. I'd rather not say any more at this time."

His "at this time" encouraged me to hope for future conversations.

I told him about Peter's wish to be a monk and his reservations about being blind.

"Would blindness be an impediment to his entry?"

"We're all blind, each in his own way, but if he really has a vocation, he'll be a good monk."

"He wants to meet you."

"Why?"

"You've had a great impact on his life."

Silence.

"Peter is a sensitive and intelligent young man. I think you'll like him."

"Do not presume . . . but I must try to be gentle. I'll see him, perhaps tomorrow."

Silence.

I felt he wanted to discuss something intimate and didn't know how to start. "Tell me more about your wife," I prompted.

He sighed and was quiet for a long time.

"Anne suffered from depression," he said slowly. "Especially in the winter. Someone suggested she might suffer from light deprivation. From then on she'd turn on every light in the house . . . and then came aroma healing and the house was filled with flowers. She'd grab at anything, holistic or otherwise, that would alleviate what she called her melancholia. The very word 'depression' depressed her."

"Light and flowers really helped?"

"I don't know. But they became important rituals for her, and I didn't interfere. Our home was filled with lamps and vases . . . what I believe really helped her was prayer."

He paused as if to let this register with me.

"She'd leave for the abbey and remain in church for hours praying before the tabernacle. The monks knew what was going on and would watch out for her. Old Dominic was wonderful, like a father to her. And she always somehow got through her darkness."

"What kind of prayer?"

"She wouldn't tell me. She felt it was between her and God. But Anne gave herself away because she spoke in a whisper when she prayed. She'd say the Jesus Prayer over and over. Of course, that may simply have been her mantra

into contemplative prayer. She was a natural contemplative . . . I chided her once for being gone from home for
five hours. She looked at me in amazement, 'Why John, I
couldn't have been out that long.' She never wore a watch.
It took me some convincing."

"Are you suggesting I pray?"

"Have you tried therapy or medication?"

"They might work for others, but I can't abide therapists and pills only made it worse for me."

He laughed.

"Why are you laughing?"

"Because Anne felt the same way."

"So it's back to prayer. You've already figured out my
agnosticism. So what's left?"

"You say my poetry helped you?"

"Yes, it recharged me and kept me going."

"Then you were essentially losing yourself in my
prayers."

"Your poetry is prayer?"

"I hadn't realized it until my wife pointed it out to me.
My poetry is my psalter. And the inspiration for my verse
is God."

"Peter said I missed the spirituality in your verse."

"He's right. You've read the *Hound of Heaven*?"

"Yes."

"God hounded me all my life, and I intuitively knew
this and fled by every escape route. But he was right

behind me. And all the joy I found in the beauty of the world was his gift to me and his lure because he led me right into his embrace."

"Didn't you—"

"Enough," he said suddenly. "Perhaps I've said too much. Let's go." Returning to the abbey, he now asked questions, about my life, the schools I had attended; he briefly addressed my book, describing it as competent and well written. His faint praise made me happy. He then asked me if I were married. When I said no , he said, "Too bad."

"Why too bad?" I asked.

He looked at me and shook his head and asked me if there was anyone special in my life. I told him all about Paula, my love for her, hers for me. I told him my fear of having children.

"I understand your fear. But it shouldn't keep you from marrying someone you love."

Before I could reply, the bells began to toll. We'd reached the circle where the retreatants had parked their cars. He handed me a folded paper. "I wrote this not long after I entered the hermitage. It will fill you in on some of the issues I was grappling with both as a poet and a monk."

After lunch I met Andrew in the conference room. He was sitting in a square of sunlight, looking out the window. His stillness touched me and I decided not to disturb him. But he heard me and turned to wave me over.

"Pete told you?" he said.

"About meeting the abbot about entering, yes."

Andrew shook his head. I sat down across from him. Silence.

"I thought you'd be happy," I said finally.

"I'm not convinced he has a vocation." Afraid of betraying a confidence, I refrained from mentioning Peter's own doubts about his vocation.

"Was Peter always a pious person?"

"Not particularly. We never missed Sunday Mass and Peter always read his New Testament. But other than that he wasn't noticeably religious."

"He has a contemplative nature, doesn't he?"

Andrew laughed. Growing up, Peter and he were total opposites, he said. Andrew was outgoing, loved sports, and won several high school letters. Peter was musical and spent most of his time at practicing the piano or reading.

"My mother would try to coax Pete from the piano—but she never succeeded. She considered it unhealthy for a boy to stay indoors so much. And Pete loved books, especially poetry. He dragged me to more recitals and poetry readings than I care to remember. Well, it wasn't so bad . . . my brother's passions have enriched my life too."

He recalled a poetry reading given by Seamus Heaney. "The hall was packed. Peter was nearly blind and insisted on sitting in the front row. We somehow squeezed into the pew, to the annoyance of the early arrivals. Heaney is a

showman and regaled the audience with a few anecdotes
before his reading. Peter was captivated. And afterwards
when Heaney agreed to sign books, Peter was the first in
line. Heaney observed me helping Peter up the stairs so he
knew Peter couldn't see well. It was ironic that the book
that Peter carried to be signed was Heaney's *Seeing Things*.
They both talked for five minutes to the annoyance of
those behind us. Peter was on cloud nine for weeks."

Andrew enjoyed telling me the story. But it was Peter's
story, I felt, and Andrew was a mere spectator. He had
dangerously submerged his identity in Peter's life which
would surely lead, I was certain, to resentment.

"Let him live his own life even if it involves making
mistakes," I said, voicing my opinion without weighing its
implications.

Andrew looked startled and his eyes watered, "He's
suffered so much and I don't—"

"It's his suffering and not yours," I said, plunging into
matters that weren't my concern. "Let him go."

Andrew vigorously shook his head as if the very idea
of leaving his brother were too much to bear.

"Perhaps," I said, "you're the one who's looking for an
escape. Having second thoughts about marriage?"

"No, I'm not," he said angrily. "Are you married?"

I shook my head.

"And you're advising me!"

Silence.

None of this was my business. My life was a shambles. I was depressed, had produced no writing since my book on Seegard, had become an ineffectual teacher, and other than Paula I had no social life.

"Please accept my apology," I said, preparing to depart.

"I'm sorry . . . please stay."

"Look, Andrew, I don't like to interfere in people's lives. But there's something about this place and you and your brother that makes me . . . makes me care about you. I'd like to think that we're friends and—"

"We are friends."

"Then as a friend let me say that I think you both need to live your own lives. It's time to separate, and parting is painful in the beginning, but it'll be the best thing for the both of you."

Andrew smiled and thanked me and said he'd seriously think about what I said.

Back in my room, I recorded in my journal my conversation with Seegard and then I read his poem; its theme was the sacrifice of silence and solitude to success and its detrimental effect on creativity. It got me thinking about Seegard's fame which surely had its annoying problems. But he was an important poetic voice, and I felt compelled to convince him that hiding his talent in a hermitage was an act of selfishness. One that wouldn't be condoned by the New Testament.

Yes, that's the argument I'll use to persuade him to resume publishing his verse and to permit me to write his biography. If Gerard Manley Hopkins had published his poetry, I'd argue, when he was alive, so many baffling questions (especially those concerning the terrible sonnets) could've been answered and scholars wouldn't be reduced to mere speculation.

It was clear, however, that when he wrote this poem, he hadn't integrated the dual roles of the poet and monk in his life. Thus far the monk was winning.

Peter was ecstatic when I told him Seegard would meet him on Saturday. I offered to accompany him to the hermitage and later to return to escort him back to the retreat house.

"Oh, don't leave me alone with him!"

"So who's the fraidy cat now?"

He laughed, but he was serious and wouldn't allow me to leave him alone with the poet. A nervous tic pulled the corner of his mouth down into a spasmodic twitch. He was more anxious about the prospect of meeting Seegard than I'd been. Perhaps he was a frightened man, and I wondered if he, indeed, were entering New Rievaulx as a haven. And if Seegard perceived this, I hoped he'd be gentle with Peter.

After None we set out for a walk. As we made our way, Peter asked me to describe everything to him: sky, hills, trees, color of leaves, texture of bark. In the middle of my descriptions, he said, "Listen, do you hear the leaves?"

"Leaves?"

"The autumn leaves sound like crinkling paper."

"And summer leaves," I asked intrigued, "how do they sound?"

"Like cascading water," he said.

We walked on.

"This is like the first time I met my father," he confessed. "He'd separated from my mother when I was an infant, and I didn't meet him until I was ten."

He paused, caught up in the memory of the past.

"Was it a disappointment?"

"No, my father took me in his arms and wept. I cried too. But Andrew was another story; he was angry and wouldn't let my father near him."

"Well, tomorrow don't expect Seegard to embrace you. He's a brusque man, but beneath it all he's a kind man." I half believed what I said. Seegard was an enigma to me.

We passed Father Dominic's bench and started down the leaf strewn path toward the stream. Peter spoke more about his life, about going blind. He admitted to a brief temptation to end his life, but the thought of how such an act would affect his family stopped him—that and his Catholic conscience.

"I decided to accept the inevitable. But before I was totally blind I soaked in the world. When I was in Paris, I spent every day at the Louvre where I absorbed all the great art I could take in. Then it occurred to me that all art is an imitation of life so I went everywhere and gazed upon everything . . . every morning I was like Adam, newly born with the whole world before me."

I described to him the panorama of hills and sky and the pond in the distance. Peter became excited by a sound I couldn't hear. "It's geese," he said, "don't you hear them?"

"Where?"

He pointed to the northwest and sure enough in the distance appeared the flying V of geese on their way south. As they flew over, I watched Peter's face, totally still and attentive. When they were gone, he smiled and resumed his remarks without losing a beat.

"What I loved looking at most was people's faces."

"Faces?"

"Someone said every face is proof of God's existence. I believe it. I've never told this to anyone, but not being able to look into people's faces, to see into their eyes . . . I miss that the most."

"You can't see faces, yet you still believe in God."

"Although I can't see them, the faces are still there. Same with God."

"That satisfies you?"

"It suffices."

Silence.

"Are you smiling at me, John?"

"No, thinking."

"Tell me what you're thinking."

"Well, I'm wondering if Seegard will suffice. We've both built him up in our minds, and no one can possibly live up to our expectations."

"If I could see his face, I'd know so much about him."

"Don't be so sure. There's no art to find the mind's construction in the face.'"

"Seegard's verse is filled with light and if it's in the verse, it's in the man."

"Then why are you so nervous about meeting him."

"I fear what he'll see in my face."

The hermitage was in sight, and out of nowhere I found myself saying, "We're near Seegard's hermitage. . . . Why not drop in on him now." Peter's grip on my arm tightened. Joined to his fear by touch, I felt the paralyzing terror of another person.

Peter objected, but I gently persuaded him that it was better to face his fear, to take the bull by the horns. What I really wanted, I realized, was to catch Seegard off guard. And I was just as scared as Peter.

Seegard met us at the door. His face looked flushed; he was likely, I concluded, sitting too close to the hearth fire. The room was indeed hot. Peter offered his hand. Seegard grabbed and shook it; he scrutinized Peter's face and invited us to sit at the kitchen table. He asked him how he became blind. Peter answered calmly and briefly. He also explained his growing desire to know God and to devote himself to a religious life. But he had reservations, "How can I be sure I'm not making a huge mistake?"

Seegard stared at Peter, and I couldn't determine his reaction to Peter's question. As the silence grew, I feared our drop-in visit was a mistake.

"I'm not a prophet, not even a wise man . . . I'm afraid I can't offer counsel to either of you."

"But you can offer an opinion," Peter said, his voice tinged with desperation.

"Yes, I could. But you may not like what you'll hear."

Peter's face drained of color. He sat as still as a statue. I looked at Seegard and my eyes begged him to be gentle. But he ignored me.

"I see a talented young man who's running away from life. A man who thinks he has a vocation to be a monk when he is really seeking safety. A safe place for blind people where he won't trip over things, and if he does there'll always be a kind monk nearby to rescue him."

"That's not true! I want to give God all that I am."

"Including your blindness?"

Peter's eyes filled with tears. "Yes, including my blindness."

Seegard stood and glared at us.

"You ask me to advise you? Well, I can't." He looked at me. "I can't solve your depression," and looking at Peter, "and I can't cure your blindness. All I can say about life is contained in my poetry and other than that I have nothing more for either of you—except—" He paused. "Except to say, pray."

"Pray?" Peter said.

"Quite frankly that is all and everything—and it's the best I can do. Take it or leave it."

He then began to laugh hysterically. I thought he'd gone mad. Peter looked lost and confused. He stood to leave when Seegard said, "Sit down, young man, I'm not finished with you."

"But I've heard enough. I want to return to the retreat house."

"No!" Seegard bellowed. I was frightened. Seegard looked unhinged. Then I saw an empty bottle of wine on the kitchen counter.

"You come here and invade my life knowing full well I'm a hermit, that I've chosen a solitary life—you both come anyway with your puny problems and disturb my peace and now you want to leave. Not yet, my young friend."

He went into the kitchen. Peter whispered that he was frightened. I explained that Seegard had been drinking.

"I know, I can smell it."

Seegard heard him. "So you've smelled my mortality? How fortunate for you. Yes, I'm only a man just like you."

He set a bottle of wine on the table along with three glasses. He poured wine and proposed a toast. Holding up his glass, he said, "To my young friends, Peter and John. For John, I pray that he'll find peace in his heart, that he'll no longer be plagued by depression. For Peter I pray that he'll find his true vocation. If God wishes him to be a monk, so be it. And now," he paused and tears glistened in his eyes, "to my dear departed wife, Anne, who died this day twelve years ago. To my dear love, may she rest in peace."

We drank. He sat down and stared at Peter.

Silence.

"Forgive me, Peter . . . today was not a good day. I got thinking about my wife and, well, I became melancholic. But I detect a problem and I would like to address it when I . . . when I'm feeling better. Do you mind if we talk tomorrow?"

"I'm sorry I intruded; I've no right to trouble you."

"I disagree, you have every right. I am your brother-in-Christ. I do wish to speak with you—tomorrow as we planned, is that acceptable?"

"Yes, thank you."

He turned to me. "And you, John. You still want to write my biography?"

"Yes, I do."

"Then, we'll talk tomorrow and I'll tell you all you need to know. In the morning as usual. As for Peter, tomorrow let's have a picnic lunch down by the pond . . . I'll take care of everything."

I was totally baffled by this sudden turn of events, but I decided it was best to let everything play itself out. Anyway, I couldn't think of anything else to do.

We went immediately to the refectory. Peter looked faint and I gave him water and told him to breathe deeply. His color slowly returned.

"You okay?"

"The wine went to my head."

"Oh, you don't drink?"

"Rarely." Then he began to laugh. "Were you as frightened as I was?"

"Probably. He had me going for a while."

"You, at least, could see his face, I was totally confused but—" He paused. "I think I like him."

"You like people who scare the hell out of you?"

"I heard in his voice a kindness, a gentleness and—"

"Gentleness!"

"Yes. When his voiced cracked at the mention of his wife, I was no longer afraid."

"I didn't hear his voice crack."

"It did. Yes, I like him and I believe he'll help me."

"It doesn't bother you that he was a bit inebriated?"

"Why should it, he's human like all of us. I think, John, you may have placed Seegard on a higher pedestal than I have." I was about to respond when Andrew arrived. We told him about Seegard's invitation to a picnic. I left the two of them animatedly talking about Seegard.

saturdaymorning

After Mass I went directly to the hermitage. I knocked twice before he answered the door. He looked hungover with deep dark circles under his eyes.

"I overslept and haven't said Mass yet. You'll be my server."

Together we stood before the altar, made of ash wood and coated in polyurethane. I was surprised I remembered the Mass responses. He recited the prayers in a voice stripped of inflection, in a diction so pure I couldn't read any of his feelings into them. His whole self was focused on the celebration of the Mass, even the turning of a page of the sacramentary was an act of utter attention.

At the approach of the Consecration, an intensification of attention arose until he was seemingly unconscious of my presence. Leaning over the bread and wine, he enunciated every word of the Consecration as if each syllable were a cut jewel. Then in the raising of the host and the chalice, he was one in the becoming of the body and blood of Christ. His face was transformed.

He asked me if I wished to receive Communion. I shook my head. How could an unbeliever receive? A part of me longed to pray, "I believe, Lord, help my unbelief." But I dismissed my longing as mere nostalgia.

I couldn't dismiss, however, Seegard's reverent celebration of the Mass. I recalled Father Flynn's stories of Jesuit missionaries who converted more Japanese by the beauty of the Mass than by their preaching. The Japanese delight in flower arrangements, haiku, zazen, and the tea ceremony; they saw the Mass as poetry in motion.

After Mass we sat on the porch drinking coffee. I complimented him on the way he said Mass.

"You found it aesthetically pleasing?"

"Yes, I did."

"You know, I could care less."

He looked at me without belligerence.

"But the church has always valued beauty," I said.

"Yes, I understand. For me the beauty is Christ, the source of all beauty."

"Christ is a presence to you?"

"He's here now. You don't believe that, do you?"

"Well, I want to believe it but . . . but I'm here to discuss you and your biography, not my lack of belief."

He laughed. He was tired and probably would've returned to bed except for my presence. But the end of the retreat was near, and this was perhaps my last chance to have him speak about himself, and I didn't want to become sidetracked by spiritual direction aimed at me.

"Tell me more about your wife?" I asked, hoping this would lead him into addressing his poetry.

He straightened and smiled.

"She was the best thing that ever happened to me."

He spoke in a low voice.

"I met her at one of my lectures at Harvard when I was awarded a chair in literature. Usually I declined such honors but I needed the money. After a lecture on Robinson Jeffers, I attended a sherry hour offered by a local maven. I usually avoid such affairs. Since you work in academia, you know how important these socials can be to one's career. Anyway a young woman with startling red hair, freckled skin, and sparkling blue eyes approached me. She identified herself as a poet and my inner radar went insane, fearing she had sneaked in a manuscript of poems for me to read. But she charmed me right off by asking me if I'd like to join her for a beer at an Irish pub in nearby Brighton where they played Irish music every night. Well, we went off to the pub and had a great time. That's how our love began."

"No talk of poetry?" I asked.

"That's all we talked about! But she could care less about my opinion for she was quite certain her verse was top-notch. Unlike you and Peter, she said my verse missed greatness because it was too vague. She was right, of course. I think my verse tends to be nebulous. I write about the sun, but she writes about the sunbeam on a bluebell's petal. See? But we both shared a love for nature. In that regard we were both Wordsworthian."

"Meaning?"

"Meaning we believed in the power of nature to restore. See, when I met Anne, my first wife, Evelyn, had been dead for some time. I thought I'd never love a woman like that again. Anne's lust for life reinvigorated me. When she asked me to marry her, she—"

"She asked you!"

"Yes, so very like her. But there was one condition. If we were to marry, we'd have to move to New Hampshire where she'd been born and raised. This presented a problem for me. Ever since I moved from California I'd experienced a writer's block. I felt I must return to my home. But she convinced me that New Hampshire could indeed be my muse as it was hers.

"Again she was right. We purchased ten acres of land not far from here. Anne knew all the monks and daily attended Mass at the abbey. She tried to convince me to accompany her, but I was a diehard agnostic. She liked to call me an unbelieving believer. When I asked her what she meant by that, she laughed and advised me to read my own verse. She'd say, 'Honey, read it closely with your eyes wide open.'

"One Easter her mother was visiting us. I went to Mass with them at the abbey. The beauty of the abbey and the

Mass moved me more than I expected, but I sloughed it all off as an aesthetic experience. After Mass, the monks crowded around Anne and her mom. She was like a daughter to many of the older monks. While they joked and gossiped, I stood aside and watched. Old Father Dominic, whose stone face revealed nothing, took pity on me and engaged me in conversation. He said he'd read all my books. At first I was flattered. Then he described me as a poet in search of God. Well, that took me by surprise and I unkindly dismissed his comment, informing him I was an agnostic. He laughed in my face and I said, 'You have something against agnostics?' He said, 'Yes, I don't much like the lukewarm. Why not take the plunge and be either hot or cold.' I was furious and about to reply when Anne wisely intervened.

"Had Dominic detected something in me that was indeed true? See, I'd rejected God and religion many years before, but when you write, you don't realize that the unconscious has a way of sneaking things into your work of which you're completely unaware. Anne understood this. My verse was my inner autobiography and close readers saw much about me that I couldn't see.

"Anne, however, kept her silence when it came to religion. But she didn't have to say a word. She was a living saint. Don't get me wrong, she wasn't a holy card saint with hands folded and eyes rolled toward heaven. She was an earthy woman whose Franciscan spirituality imbued her life and her poetry. Living with that before you is like being before an icon."

"Her poetry?"

"It's a blend of New England and Ireland. She's Yankee on her father's side and Irish Catholic on her mother's. Her verse is a rare blend of Emersonian transcendentalism and Catholic mysticism. God was a living presence to her. She wrote about the radiance of nature's diminutives, the shape and color of a pebble, a curiously twisted twig, the contour of a bird's egg, a leaf lying in rainwater, or a bright dewdrop dangling atop a blade of grass, things most of us miss."

"William Blake says, 'Everything that is is holy'."

"Yes, that's how she saw it . . . and because of her I began to question my lack of belief. She saw this change in me and encouraged me to talk with Father Dominic. We argued about his suitability, but she insisted that he was my intellectual match. "He'll give you a run for your money," she said. To my surprise Dominic and I became fast friends."

"And did he convert you?"

"For over a year we met and discussed everything from science to poetry to theology. He was a brilliant man who'd been educated in England. He won a Greats at Oxford. Yes, he was an intellectual whom I respected. But he couldn't bring me into the fold, although to be fair to him I don't think it really was his goal. He wasn't prone to proselytizing. He was simply there for me. An act of kindness. Yes, I was indeed searching for God—or rather God was searching for me—and I hadn't admitted this to anyone. It was my one repression."

"Repression?"

"Freud theorized that man's most harmful repression concerned human sexuality. I believe, however, that the great repression of our time is that of the spiritual impulse."

"I see."

"Do you?"

He smiled a knowing smile which annoyed me.

"What about Father Dominic?"

"We had a heated argument about religion and science and I angrily said, 'Can you prove scientifically the existence of God?' Dominic calmly rejoined, 'Can you scientifically prove the nonexistence of God?' His question was like the solution to a Zen *koan* to me. In an instant I was freed. A moment of *satori*. Tears sprung to my eyes and I began to weep. Poor Dominic was at a loss; he came to me and embraced me, afraid that somehow he had hurt my feelings."

"What did happen?"

"My eyes were opened. For years my rational mind categorically ruled out the possibility of the transcendent. All in the name of science. But science never could explain the things that are important to me. For instance, it can't explain the world's beauty by which I had lived my life. Or explain love. Dominic's question was the beginning of my conversion."

"There's a great distance between conversion and becoming a Cistercian monk."

"Not really. When Anne died, I had to decide what to do with the rest of my life. Having finally discovered God, I felt drawn to know more, and by knowing I mean intimately. Of course, it wasn't so much my decision as God's."

"So you were certain you had a vocation?"

"After Anne died, I went through a paralyzing grief. But gradually my spiritual life became deeper. Naturally I thought I might be escaping sorrow by entering a monastery. I explained this to Abbot Raines, who is a wise man. He helped me to see that I had a religious vocation."

"So someone can help?"

He paused as if struck by a revelation. "Ah, Peter?"

"Peter needs you."

"Yes, I think you're correct . . . and I need Peter."

I hadn't expected this.

"Why do you need Peter?"

"God has sent him to me, and I'll not make the same mistake twice."

Seegard became still and had gently turned his head toward the stream . A doe and her fawn had arrived at the stream. We watched them and time seemed to stop. Then they lifted their heads, remained still for a while, and darted back into the woods.

"They often come here for the water. Miraculous, aren't they?"

They were, but afraid to lose the momentum of our interview, I said, "You referred to the young poet. You wish to speak about him?"

"Yes, it's time I face this and make—"

"Make?"

"Make atonement for the way I treated him."

Silence.

"Tell me about it," I gently prodded.

"Yes, perhaps I should finally put this to rest."

He took a deep breath and exhaled.

"He was a young postulant Anne had become friendly with . . . she enjoyed taking the monks out on picnics on the abbey grounds. One Sunday she tricked me into going with her. When we arrived at the abbey, Brother Matthew was waiting for us. A pleasant enough fellow, but I should've been forewarned, for he held in his hand a manila envelope. We were lunching by the pond on a flawless summer day. I was unscrewing the thermos of coffee when I caught Anne's signal to him. He asked me to read some of his poems.

"I was angered by her little subterfuge. The monks were her friends and if one wanted a professional opinion about poems, then she should've offered it. Anyway, I read the poems and they were awful, pious drivel and I said so. He seemed to take my criticism well. When he asked me if I thought he had any talent, I told him I didn't detect any. I softened my remarks by saying that perhaps with practice he could write good poetry.

"Anne and I had our first row over this. She accused me of cruelty. I accused her of setting me up. She was a fine poet in her own right and should've advised the young man. She countered that he had asked for me to read his poetry and not her.

"Several months later Matthew left the monastery. Anne was so depressed by this. She blamed herself for his departure. Shortly after, we learned that he'd taken his life."

"But surely you don't blame yourself!"

"I didn't at first. I convinced myself that he was a neurotic. Anne thought otherwise, and it caused a lot of tension between us. Then I received a letter addressed to me by Matthew. His parents found it among his belongings. He said I destroyed his dream of being a contemplative and a poet. He described me as an expert in cruelty and said that I should devote the rest of my life to learning gentleness."

"He wasn't well."

"Yes, but he spoke the truth. See, Matthew impressed me with his gentleness. But that didn't stop me from mauling him."

"How did your wife react to the letter?"

"I never showed it to her. So now you understand. I don't want to make the same mistake with Peter . . . or with you."

"I'm not about to take my life over anything you say!"

"You think so? I saw your face the first day you came here."

"In that case I'm glad you changed your mind," I said. "One would think that being gentle would be the easiest thing in the world."

"Yes, one would think. I pray for gentleness every day of my life. Gentleness with others . . . and even with myself."

It was time to prepare this afternoon's lunch. He appeared to be happy by the prospect. "It's been a long time since I've picnicked . . . I look forward to it."

So did I.

saturdayafternoon

When Peter and I arrived at the hermitage, Seegard was sitting on the porch reading his breviary. When he saw us, he made the sign of the cross and disappeared inside. Humming a tune, he was packing what looked like a substantial lunch.

"Glad the weather is warm enough, but you've wisely worn sweaters."

We followed him down a winding path strewn with autumn leaves.

Peter's grip on my arm was tight. "Relax, Peter, and enjoy the day," I whispered, sure that Seegard wouldn't hear. "You're having a picnic with Ethan Seegard, would you ever have imagined it?"

He smiled. "Sound's like he's in a much better mood."

"Yesterday was the wine."

"Went to my head too," he said, laughing.

Seegard had reached a grassy level of ground near the pond's bank. After he spread out the blanket for us, he opened a beach chair for himself. Peter and I sat cross-legged on the ground. Seegard unpacked the basket, a cornucopia of food: broiled chicken, tomatoes and cucumber, stuffed eggs, Quiche Lorraine, Camembert and crackers, French bread, butter, apples, grapes, oranges, apple tarts, a bottle of red wine, and a thermos of coffee.

"There's enough food for an army," I said.

"Well, eat as much as you like."

We ate in silence. It was somewhat awkward, and I wanted to break the ice but was unsure as to how to begin. Seegard gazed out toward the pond, a calm blue oval of water.

"I remember when I had my interview with Abbot Raines," Seegard said, still gazing at the water. "He put me through the third degree and I feared the community would reject my candidacy."

"So you weren't a shoo-in," I said.

"Why would I be?"

"A famous poet, well, you'd think they'd be honored to have you."

Seegard laughed. "You don't know monks very well. Fame means nothing here."

"Then what was the abbot's third degree about?"

Seegard looked at Peter, who was still and attentive. He aimed his every word at Peter.

"He peeled me like an onion, layer after layer until he was satisfied that I wasn't doing the right thing for wrong reason."

We'd finished the bottle of wine. Seegard unscrewed the coffee thermos and poured three cups.

"How did you know you had a vocation?"

"You cut to the chase, Peter. I like that."

Seegard looked out toward the water. He knew how important his answer was for Peter, and he measured his words carefully.

"I fell in love with Christ. It's that simple. And I wanted to dedicate the rest of my life to him."

"But you can love Christ in the world, too," Peter said.

"True, but I wanted to give myself totally and that meant sacrificing something for Christ. See, I believe in sacrifice. By coming here I gave up a lot, though of course it may appear self-serving, for much of what I renounced I had no use for anyway."

"Fame?" I said.

"Yes, it becomes wearisome after a while. But there were other things."

"Then you had no doubt God was calling you to this life?" Peter asked.

"My attraction to monastic life was so strong that I believed God was indeed calling me. Is it that way with you, Peter?"

Peter was quiet for a while before he answered.

"I tend to be overanalytical," he said. "On some days I'm so certain God wants me here but then on other days I'm overwhelmed with doubt."

"Listen to your inner voice," Seegard said. "But you perhaps won't know for sure until you spend some time here."

"What if the committee refuses me because I'm blind?"

"They won't," Seegard said.

"How can you be so certain?"

"Because I'm on the candidates' committee."

Peter smiled nervously. "Have I already done myself in?"

"Look, Peter, you won't be rejected for your blindness. Our community is quite liberal about the kinds of people it lets in. We'd like to be a microcosm of the world. Unlike some religious communities, we don't make candidates take a battery of tests in search of the perfect monk or nun. A monastery should be a reflection of the world. We have our fair share of the wounded both physically and psychologically here at New Rievaulx. They arrive here, and most stay for a short time and depart. Then there are those who remain until death."

"So even I have a chance to become a monk," I said to lighten things.

"We have monks who suffer from depression," he said, clearly annoyed by my flippancy. "But within the structure of our monastic life with its focus on prayer and work, they are able to live as good monks."

"But if it were known beforehand," I said, "would I be allowed in?"

"That would depend on the makeup of the committee. The one we currently have would at the least allow you to test your vocation."

He then turned to Peter and said, "Peter, there is no easy answer. Pray. God will show you what to do."

"Yesterday you said I was escaping life. Why have you changed your mind?"

"That was unfair of me. I believe our community will be able to help you come to a decision. That's why we have a postulancy, to help people discover whether or not they truly have a vocation."

Peter thanked Seegard for his kind counsel. We set to finishing the rest of the lunch. Peter who had formerly picked at his food now ate with appetite.

Seegard recalled the first time he came here to this pond's edge.

"I'd finished my interview with the abbot. To allow everything he said to sink in, I walked down to the edge of the water. It was so beautiful. I watched the loons glissade over its surface. No wind. No sound. Deep silence. I knew then and there that I must learn to know this silence, to become its friend, to make it a part of my being—therein lay my salvation. And I prayed that Abbot Raines would accept me."

"Your prayer was answered," Peter said.

"Yes, it's a good thing to pray."

Peter nodded and quietly said, "I do."

Seegard looked closely at Peter and reached out to pat his shoulder. While we were quietly sitting, I imagined us in a three-paneled painting: at the center was a radiantly wise Seegard standing at a lector, reading; at his feet there were two disciples; on his right, one bathed in golden light and on his left, one clouded in shadow. I had no doubt about which one I was.

Then Seegard cleared his throat, his signal to pack up and depart. As we prepared to leave, Seegard looked at the both of us and said, "Has any of what I've said been helpful?"

I smiled and Peter nodded and Seegard said, "Good."

Since we were leaving tomorrow, we made our farewells at the hermitage. Seegard embraced me and consented to my writing his biography. He said I'd hear from his lawyer, granting me legal permission to access all his private papers housed here at the abbey. He embraced Peter and said he'd be around to help him during his postulancy. Peter was grateful, "But I don't want any preferential treatment."

"Don't worry," said Seegard, "around here no one gets preferential treatment. Not even a poet." He laughed.

saturdayeveningbeforevespers

I took my usual stall. The church was empty. Vespers wouldn't be for another hour. Ever since I was a kid I loved quiet places like churches and libraries; they were oases in a crowded and noisy city. I especially liked libraries where people were silent but also working, either reading or studying or writing. Libraries, however, were never as quiet as this abbey church. And this silence was different. I was no connoisseur of silence, but I knew this was different. But how it was different I couldn't articulate.

Tomorrow I leave the abbey. One week here and my life has changed. I'd met the poet I most admire. I may have made a friend in him. And he'd given me permission to write his biography. I'd accomplished what I set out to do. It felt good. And I made friends with Peter and Andrew. Surely my life has been enriched. Why then am I sad? It's not depression. No, it's not that. More like regret, and I must try to understand this unexpected emotion.

The monastery is beautiful, and the monks are good people. Yes, life is indeed beautiful here. My academic life, unfortunately, rarely achieves such beauty. How could it when it's a Byzantine court of intrigue and politics, of who's in and who's out. Here at New Rievaulx everyone's "in."

Such had been my thoughts as I sat in the silence of the abbey church roughly an hour before Saturday's Vespers. Then like Paul on the road to Damascus, I heard my name spoken: "John Highet." A chill shot through me. I again heard my name, and my heart began to pound. I thought someone, Peter perhaps, might be calling me so I stood and looked around the church, but I saw no one.

I stepped into the aisle and looked toward the sanctuary. There lying on the floor of the middle aisle was a monk stretched crosswise. It was the mudra of total Christian obeisance. I'd seen priests do this when I was a young altar boy. Had my name emanated from that white pile? I stared in fascination and not too much time passed by when again I heard my name. Someone was praying for me. I was moved and humbled. Tears sprung to my eyes. That someone would storm heaven about me—it was too much to bear.

How many times in my life had I heard someone say, "I'll pray for you." People say it but don't really mean it. Like the garage attendant who asked me to pray for him and I consented but really had no intention to offer even a "Glory be" for him. And here was a monk spread out on the floor, praying for me—unbidden.

For a moment I thought it might be Seegard. But the monk's length didn't add up to Seegard's height. So I watched for I don't know how long. Then the prostrate form began to arise. And slowly. My fancy conjured up a phoenix rising from its white ashes. First to his knees. The cowl's hood was up so I couldn't see the face. Then swaying from right to left, the figure rose to his two feet, his white robed arms spread like wings steadying himself. Fully erect, he dropped his arms and stood before the tabernacle for several more minutes. Then he made the sign of the cross and pushed down his hood.

Abbot Raines.

I kept silent. He couldn't see me as I was in darkness and partially hidden by a pillar. Abbot Raines praying for me. I felt honored and could've wept for the mere kindness of the man, for his concern, and—for his love.

I had no doubt for what he'd prayed.

sundaymorning

S unday Mass was a concelebrated Mass with twenty
monks half-circling the altar. Clouds of incense transformed the sanctuary into a scene out of medieval times.
Both side chapels overflowed with locals. At Communion
there wasn't a person in the church who didn't receive.
Except me. There were some furtive glances toward me
from the retreatants. I can't say I wasn't embarrassed, but
back at the refectory everyone was kind and in an effusive
mood; we all talked about the beauty of New Rievaulx, the
retreat, and the Mass.

Saying good-bye to Andrew and Peter was hard, but
we exchanged addresses and telephone numbers and
made promises to stay in touch. Peter said his address
starting in January would be New Rievaulx. I congratulated
Andrew on his upcoming wedding.

"You know about it?" Peter said.

"Yes, Andrew told me when—"

Peter turned to his brother, "You didn't tell me John
knew."

Andrew was shaken, and I knew I made a faux pas.

"I was anxious about how you'd take it, and I needed someone to talk to."

"Anxious?"

"We've rarely been apart, Pete. I'm your brother, and I've a right to be anxious about someone I love."

His "I love" deflated what nearly had turned into a tense scene. Peter reached out for his brother's hand.

"I understand."

He turned to me, "John, you're good at keeping secrets. That'll come in handy as a biographer."

"How's that?"

"No biographer should tell everything he learns about his subject."

"Why?"

"Some things are best left to God. But that's a discussion for another time."

We embraced and I helped carry their luggage to their car. We embraced again, and I watched them drive off in their small Lumina. Watched until they disappeared around the bend.

Returning to the retreat house to book a retreat, I met Abbot Raines. Not a chance meeting, I suspected.

"Ah, Mr. Highet. I'm glad to see you and pleased that you stayed the course of our retreat. Did you get all that you need?"

"Yes, Reverend Father, that and more."

"I gather that we will be seeing more of you in the future?"

"Yes, I've received permission from Ethan Seegard to write his biography."

"Well, Mr. Highet, I'm sure you are well qualified to write Father Aelred's biography. But if you return here as a scholar, I will still require your attending our liturgical hours and our daily Mass. Are you willing to do that?"

"Do I have a choice?"

He began to laugh and I thought he'd let me off the hook.

"I'm a firm believer in free will. The choice is all yours, as long as you understand what the choice is."

"And that is?"

He smiled. "You may come or not come to New Rievaulx. If you come, you'll attend all services."

Abbot Raines was a man of steel, and I knew there'd be no compromise. But succumbing to his demands was easy. I knew what he was up to.

"Is it a deal, Mr. Highet?"

"Yes, Reverend Father, it's a deal."

He reached out and shook my hand and wished me a safe return to Boston.

I found Jerome in his office. I stood in the door for a while before he realized I was there.

"Mr. Highet, may I help you?" he said, smiling. The first smile I'd received from him. Now because I'm leaving?

"I'd like to book a retreat, sometime in the next two or three months."

"You would?" he said, sounding surprised.

"Yes. Is my request unusual?"

"Well, I would've thought you got what you came here for . . . to meet Ethan Seegard, correct?"

"How did you know?"

"When you arrived, I noticed Father Aelred's *Collected Poetry* sticking out of your bag. So I assumed you were another journalist snooping around for a story."

"Well, part of that is true, Father Jerome. I'm sorry that I wasn't on the level about being here. But I sincerely want to book a retreat."

He said, "I've been too harsh, please forgive me, but I understand how much Father Aelred values solitude, and I don't like to see anyone take advantage of him."

We finalized a date for a retreat, and he carried my luggage to my car. We shook hands and off I went. I could see him in my rear view mirror still waving good-bye.

A few days later I met Paula at Starbuck's for coffee. The first thing she said was that I looked different.

"You've changed," she said, studying me.

"Oh, in what way?"

"Your eyes, it's in your eyes."

"Have they changed color or are they still blue?" I asked, amused by Paula's fancy.

"They're not blue stones anymore." She smiled and patted my hand.

"So if the stones are gone," I said, taking her hand in mine, "what do you see now?"

She looked deeply into my eyes and said, "I see blue . . . blue hope."

"Hope?"

"Yes, that's what I see," she said. She sipped her coffee and grimaced, "Coffee is cold."

I went to the counter and returned with a hot mug of coffee.

"Cream?" I asked, knowing full well she'd refuse.

"Don't be foolish. I have my figure to consider," she said and laughed at her own vanity. She then put on the table a Barnes and Noble bag.

"This is for you."

"Ah, a book." I took it out.

"Hildegarde von Bingen!"

"You're not angry?"

"No. Though it is a bit of humble pie, I admit. You had every right to remind me of my roots. And as Peter Huxley says, I must read Hildegarde in order to better understand Seegard. This will help me make a start. Thank you."

"You're welcome."

"Paula? How is it that you do or say the very thing I need?"

"Oh, I don't know. It likely falls under the rubric of love."

A declaration of love was expected, but I found myself saying, "Sounds like a good title for a book: *Rubric of Love.* . . ."

"Yes, and how clever of you to avoid saying—"

"I love you? Must I say it?"

"Love, you already have."

Paula's birthday was coming up. Her favorite poet is Christina Rossetti and for a long time I'd been searching for a first edition of *Goblin Market*.

Through Alibris I located it. I planned to give that and a card as gifts.

We'd begun a tradition of celebrating her birthday at the Harvest in Cambridge, a restaurant Paula enjoyed for both its quiet ambience and nouveau cuisine. She discovered it after attending a matinee at the Cambridge Repertory's production of Chekhov's *The Cherry Orchard*. And the fact that Julia Child was seated at the next table convinced her that she'd chosen well.

I'd been waiting for her at the bar, sipping a Merlot. I'd only been back from the monastery for a week before my depression began to rear its ugly head again. I wasn't prepared, for usually I enjoyed a more prolonged respite. This time, however, I think it had to do, in part, with my missing the abbey, the monks. The abbey's quiet and beauty exerted a positive effect on me and somehow kept my depression at bay. Perhaps it was the liturgical hours with its Lectio Divina and the daily Mass, along with the communal meals. Now that I think of it I was always doing something at the abbey. Although "doing" isn't quite the right word. *Being.* Yes, that's it. I allowed myself to be—in a way that I don't usually experience. What was the difference? I can't put my finger on it, but I suspect it had something to do with a quality of silence and of solitude.

I'd be reading in my condo or cooking a meal and I'd find myself waiting for the abbey bells to toll. Why their mellow tones possess the power to emotionally move me is baffling; perhaps it has something to do with their soothing, unhurried measurement of time or their link to some long-forgotten memory. Anyway, sitting at the bar, I was thinking about the abbey and the monks and how much I missed them, including Jerome, Seegard's faithful Cerberus, when I felt a tap on my shoulder. I turned to find Paula, who gave me a nice little smooch.

"Thank you and happy birthday," I said, giving her an added peck on the cheek. I signaled to the maitre'd who led us to Paula's favorite table by the window. She wore a white suit topped off by a blue Hermes silk scarf that, I couldn't help noticing, matched the blue of her eyeshadow. As she made her way through the maze of tables, not a few men raised their eyes. Other men's appreciation of Paula's beauty never bothered me. I felt it was her due. To be frank, I was proud that she was with me. An ego trip, I thought, but surely not one to be ashamed of.

"I sense low vibes from you, are you all right?"

"Oh, just a little low. Believe it or not, I miss the abbey and the monks."

She smiled and began to light a cigarette.

"Paula, the new city law of no restaurant smoking, remember?"

"I forgot . . . the Cambridge fanatics and their obsession with their bodies. Would they be so willing to give up their cars? Not likely. Every day they breathe in car exhaust which is polluting the whole damn city, but *I* have to give up cigarettes." She raised her voice slightly so that our neighbors could hear. Satisfied after venting her annoyance, she dutifully returned her lighter to her purse. The meal was as usual perfect, and we were now enjoying an after-dinner cognac. We talked about Seegard and my plans to begin working on his biography as soon as possible. It would mean staying at the monastery for a long period of time because his papers are housed there.

"Love, this is so good for you. But—" She reached for her glass which she slowly raised to her lips.

"But?"

She returned the glass to the table and looked intently at me.

"You sure? You won't like it."

"I can take it."

"Look, I'm delighted that Seegard's poetry has helped you and that you want to write his biography. But you're too wrapped up in books. They mean more to you than life. Books are not life but its mirror."

"It was you," I said, "who suggested that I write another book."

"Confession: It was a last ditch effort to pull you out your depression. But what if your depression is somehow related to a fear of life, and writing Seegard's biography doesn't help? We'll find ourselves right back where we started."

"Now it's *fear* of life? You're saying I'm a coward?"

"Be quiet and listen! I'm saying you've lived a vicarious life and that you don't allow yourself new experiences. You're a beautiful soul, and there is nothing wrong with loving books and devoting your attention to them. My God, we both make our living teaching young people how to read. But books aren't life, life is life—that's all I'm saying. As to Seegard, if writing his biography returns your passion for life then write it because you're the one to do it. But, dearest, don't give up on your own life . . . on our life."

I hadn't noticed that Paula had lit up a cigarette with curls of smoke rising to the ceiling. The maitre'd came over, "Madame, no smoking is allowed."

She looked at her hand, saw the offence and, gazed up at the maitre'd, "I'm very sorry, please forgive me." He nodded, bowed, and departed. Paula put out the cigarette in the bread plate. I reached over to take her hand.

"Don't worry, I'm not giving up on anything."

"You mean it?"

I nodded and then I placed my gift and card on the table, and Paula slowly unwrapped it. Her eyes welled as she tenderly opened the book.

"A first edition?" she said.

"Yes. After all these years I finally found one."

"Expensive?" she asked, gently leafing through its pages.

"I'll never tell."

"I love it," she said, "and look, some of the pages haven't been cut . . . just think of it, they've never seen the light of day."

"Don't get too wrapped up in it, now. It's only a book."

She raised her eyebrows. "You got me. Touché."

"Don't you want to read the card? I chose it carefully."

She opened the card and read the verse and looked at me, "It's perfect. But what's this?" She held in her hand a piece of paper that had fallen out.

"It's a letter I received it from Seegard."

"You want me to read it?" she asked, somewhat bemused.

"Please do."

Dear John,

I hope all is well with you. I have spoken with Abbot Raines, who has agreed to let you reside in the candidates' lodge when you return to begin your work on my biography. As I said to you, I shall offer you access to all my papers housed here at the abbey. However, I have decided not to allow anything to be removed from our archives, nor do I want any Xeroxing done of my papers. I hope this proves not to be onerous in your work. But that's the way it must be.

Do not think for a moment that I am trying to discourage you from writing my biography. You have convinced me that it must be written. I want someone I respect, someone who understands my poetry, to write it. And that person is you.

On another note: When you interviewed me, you alluded to my "source of joy." I've been thinking much about this. This may sound absurd to you, but I'm convinced that the source of joy and its opposite are one and the same. A paradox I'm at my wit's end to explain. But of late I had a breakthrough concerning this very matter, and I have learned something important about life.

I want to share this with you when you return here. It may indeed help lead you out of the maze

of your fears, freeing you to do some of the things
you have put off, such matters that relate to faith
and love and marriage.

Now before I begin to ramble on let me say
this again: I really do want you to write my biography, but you'll have to do much of it here. And if
I can be of service to you as a new friend and as a
priest, I am ready and willing. Abbot Raines said
the other day, "Mr. Highet was sent to our abbey
for a reason." I think he's right. And now we must
discover his purpose, which I suspect is far more
vital than writing my biography.

My best to you and your friend, Paula,
F. Aelred (a.k.a. Ethan Seegard)

Paula folded the letter into the card and placed it on
top of *Goblin Market*. She looked at me.

"Not bad gifts for a birthday, are they?"

"Not bad at all. As a matter of fact, I can say these are
the best birthday gifts I've received. Ever."

"Ever?"

"Yes. And to think they were chosen by someone who
once had blue stones for eyes."